This book

_____

Children's
POOLBEG

By the same author:

Where is Joe?

"The kind of book that changes attitudes."

Children's
POOLBEG

Joe in the middle

Joe in the middle
Tony Hickey

The first book in the series

POOLBEG

First published 1988 by
Poolbeg Press Ltd
Knocksedan House,
Swords, Co Dublin, Ireland
Reprinted 1991

This book is published with the assistance of
The Arts Council/An Chomhairle Ealaíon, Ireland.

ISBN 1 85371 021 0

Cover design by Robert Ballagh
Illustrated by Robert Ballagh
Printed by The Guernsey Press Company Ltd,
Vale, Guernsey, Channel Islands

For
Roisín,
Dermot
and
Cormac

Jacko

Chapter One

oe tried not to squeeze the brown paper bag as he opened the gates of the Meehan Institute for Boys and started down the long tree-lined avenue. Usually, returning to the Institute was the worst moment of the week for him, cancelling out the good time he always had with the Philipses. But on this particular evening he had no sad feelings. Instead, his whole being seemed to zing with the announcement that had been made so casually over tea. The Philipses were going to have a birthday party for him!

'We didn't like to say anything until we were sure,' Mrs Philips had said when she came back from answering the telephone. 'That was Mr Lawford giving his permission.'

A birthday party all his own! No-one at the Institute ever had a birthday party all to himself. They were always shared with other boys born around the same time. At best, they were dull affairs. At worst, they could be totally depressing with some new arrival crying for his parents.

And yet, in spite of the sadness that such tears cast over the so-called celebrations, lately Joe had begun to wonder if it wasn't better to be an orphan than to have a father like his, whom he hadn't seen for over a year now.

It had been different when Joe had first come to the Institute, eight years ago after his mother's death. Then his father had visited him every week. Then the visits had become monthly. Then they had become completely unpredictable; his father just showing up without any warning, staying a few minutes and then leaving as abruptly as he had arrived. Both Mr Lawford and Matron regarded him as a disruptive influence and would have preferred him not to visit at all.

Well, they didn't have much cause for complaint lately. Joe hadn't even had a Christmas card.

'Maybe he's forgotten me,' Joe thought and was amazed at how that idea upset him. He tried to shrug the feeling away but it persisted and, all at once, it was as though the excitement about the birthday party had never existed.

And yet it did exist. The party was all arranged, Mr Lawford had given his permission. Mrs Philips had, that very day, tried out a new cake recipe and given him some of it to bring back to the Institute. That was what was in the brown paper bag.

And anyway, what had his father to do with anything? If he could manage without Joe, Joe could certainly manage without him.

But a small nagging voice inside his head refused to leave things at that. It seemed determined to defeat every attempt Joe made to get back the feeling of happiness that, for once, had made him not mind returning to the Institute.

Joe broke into a run, ignoring the dark clouds gathering in the sky and the wind that sent the dead leaves crackling through the shrubbery. It was only when he reached the statue of Sir Joseph, founder of the Institute, that Joe slowed down. Eight years ago he'd been afraid of that statue, imagining that it might suddenly come to life and condemn him to some terrible punishment. Joe had grown out of such fears, realising that the statue of a man who had been dead for over a hundred years could not harm him. But even so, the glowering expression on the face of the statue and the overbearing set of the shoulders reminded Joe that the last thing he must do now was attract too much attention. If he seemed even remotely upset, Matron and Mr Lawford were quite capable of deciding that the party plans were having a bad effect on him and insisting that the arrangements be cancelled.

'I'll feel better when I'm indoors,' Joe thought.

But the hall, crowded with boys, was far too bright and noisy after the dark gardens and Joe felt a sudden surge of panic that he might not be able to maintain his calm exterior. He made quickly for the stairs and Dormitory Number Two where he flung himself down on his bed. But he had no sooner closed his eyes when a voice made him open them again. Charlie Morris, his best friend, was looking down at him. 'Hey, what's the matter with you? I tried to talk to you in the hall but you pushed straight past me, as though you'd seen a ghost.'

'That statue of Sir Joseph suddenly gave me the creeps.'

'That's what it's intended to do. What have you got in the bag?'

'Cake.'

'That the Philipses gave you? They must really like you. I don't think my sponsors will invite me any more. I keep banging into the furniture and stepping on the cat.'

'There's more than just the cake.' Charlie's presence was having a calming effect on Joe. There was something so reassuring about Charlie even when, as now, Joe was feeling a bit sorry for himself. Both Charlie's parents were dead and he was forever telling Joe how lucky he was to have a father no matter how seldom he heard from him. 'There's a party as well.'

'A party?' But that was all Charlie had time to say as the silhouette of Matron became visible through the frosted panels of the door.

Joe jumped up off his bed and pushed the paper bag underneath it. Matron was a stickler for discipline and one of her most strongly enforced rules was no food in the dormitories because of the danger of attracting mice.

'Oh, so this is where you are, nattering as usual. I've been looking for you, Mathews. No school tomorrow. Your father is due here in the morning.' Then, sighing at what she considered to be Joe's lack of response, she said, 'Honestly, such a boy! I sometimes wonder if you're fully awake. You do know what day it will be in three weeks' time?'

'It'll be my twelfth birthday.'

'And you do know what that means as regards staying here?'

'Yes. It means it's my last year at the Institute.'

'Mine too,' Charlie said.

'Your circumstances are quite different from those of Mathews. Arrangements for his future have to be finalised.'

'But I thought they had been finalised,' said Joe. 'I thought it was all arranged for me to go to Merton House with Charlie and the others.'

'That just goes to show how foolish it is to ever take things for granted.' She sailed out of the dormitory like a white, starched galleon in her spotless white uniform.

Joe turned to Charlie. 'What does she mean, "Your circumstances are different"?'

'She must mean your father. He'd have to agree to any arrangements that were made.'

'But surely they'd have got in touch with him before now.'

'Maybe he has to sign forms.'

'In other words, give me away officially.'

'Hey, don't get narky with me. It's not my fault if he doesn't come to see you.'

'I'm not bothered if I never heard from him again.'

'That's not true and you know it, but what's this about a party?'

'Oh, the Philipses got permission from Mr Lawford this afternoon to have a birthday party for me. I can invite six of my friends.'

Charlie's reaction was not at all as Joe had expected. Instead of being amazed, Charlie became very thoughtful. 'I wonder why he picked this afternoon to give his permission?'

'What difference does that make as long as he said "Yes"?'

'It could make a lot of difference if it's connected with your father's visit tomorrow. Supposing it was decided that you weren't to go to Merton House, where would you go instead?'

Joe suddenly knew where the conversation was leading and he backed away at once. 'You know we're not even supposed to think about such a thing much less talk about it.'

'And how do you know what I was going to say if it wasn't in your mind already?' demanded Charlie.

'I just guessed, that's all.' And yet even as he made that reply. Joe knew that what Charlie had said was true. It wasn't just the thought of the party that had overwhelmed Joe. It was the bond between himself and the Philipses, which the party represented, that was really important. The three of them were no longer just part of a social experiment designed to let the boys at the Institute experience life in a private home. He and the Philipses had become almost like a family. And if the Philipses were interested in fostering him, this would be the ideal moment for talks to take place with his father.

'He could kill two birds with the one stone,' thought Joe, bitterly. 'Wish me a happy birthday and get rid of me at the same time.'

The nagging voice was back again, questioning the sincerity of Joe's indifference to his father, and Joe did not know how to cope with these thoughts. Desperately he looked around for some distraction from the growing turmoil in his mind. 'Hey, look, it's snowing. We might have time to go out before supper. You'd better take care of the cake.'

Charlie shoved the bag up his jersey without it making any noticeable alteration to his shape and followed Joe out of the dormitory.

Other boys had had the same idea of going out into the grounds. The hall door was open. A flurry of flakes blew into the hall. Then Mr Lawford came out of the staff quarters. 'Whoever opened that door will shut it immediately. Those who are out-of-doors will return at once. Then all of you will go and sit in the day-room until supper. There will be no television this evening for anyone.' Mr Lawford, tall and thin, allowed his eyes to sweep intimidatingly over his charges. When they reached Joe their expression changed for an instant and, brief as that change was, both Charlie and Joe noticed it.

'There you are,' Charlie whispered. 'What did I tell you? Something is definitely going on. Lawford couldn't even look you in the face without giving it away.'

'Oh don't keep on about it,' Charlie's words were too like his own thoughts spoken out loud. 'Leave me alone. Feed your face with the cake. That might keep you quiet for a while.'

Charlie was stunned by what he clearly regarded as an unprovoked attack. 'I don't want your old cake,' he said. 'Here!' He thrust the cake into Joe's hand. 'Feed your own face with it.'

Those were the last words Charlie spoke to

Joe that evening and Joe just could not bring himself to apologise. To do so would be to admit, somehow, that Charlie was right when he said Joe had been hoping that the weekends with the Philipses might lead to something else.

Not that there wasn't a boy in the Institute who didn't secretly wish for a life with people who wanted him because they cared about him and not just because it was their job to look after him.

But for Joe to say so out loud was like tempting fate, counting chickens before they were hatched.

And there was his father as well. Suddenly so many things were surfacing in Joe's mind; things he had tried not to consider. Now it seemed as though they could no longer be avoided if, as Charlie had said, something was definitely going on.

Silently Joe placed the bag of cake in the middle of the supper table. He had no appetite for it. Charlie didn't touch it either but the other boys at the table had no such qualms.

Ned

Chapter Two

hat night Joe dreamed he was walking along a cliff. Overhead the sky was bright with stars. A white ship was anchored in the middle of the bay. From that ship there came the sound of a woman singing; at first quite gently but then her voice grew stronger and clearer, with a strange lilt to it:

> The road is long
> It slowly winds
> To the house we know
> So well
> And as it winds, sleep
> Well, my child,
> Tomorrow is another day.

The melody seemed to hover in the air and to be directed solely at Joe. Then it began to fade and the ground beneath Joe's feet crumbled.

Joe tried to cry out as he fell down into the darkness but no sound came. Then suddenly he was awake, staring at the pattern that the night sky made on the dormitory ceiling.

For a moment it was almost like still being in the dream, so vividly did the details of the seascape and the words of the song linger in his mind. He was certain he had never dreamed such a dream before and yet there was something familiar about it; like a scene remembered from the past, triggered off by some chance remark. Dreams could work that way. He remembered hearing Mr and Mrs Philips talking about it once. Did that mean then that the dream of the ship and of the woman singing had some connection with the party and his father's visit?

It was so difficult to imagine his father asleep out there beyond the walls of the Institute. Or was he, like Joe, awake and thinking of the future?

Joe snuggled down further under the blankets. He wished he knew what time it was. He was convinced he'd never get back to sleep. It had been a miracle that he had ever managed to sleep in the first place.

'The road is long. It slowly winds . . . . '

Maybe if he knew what the dream referred

to, he'd understand his own feelings better.

The pattern on the ceiling flickered and vanished as clouds settled across the moon. Joe drifted back into a sleep untroubled by dreams; a strangely tranquil sleep.

When he woke the dormitory was empty except for Charlie, seated on a radiator.

Joe got out of bed and made for the washbasins. 'I didn't hear the bell. And I'm sorry for the way I behaved last night.'

But the apology did nothing to change the expression in Charlie's eyes. He just shrugged and walked out of the dormitory before Joe could even attempt an explanation of how complicated his thoughts had been.

In the dining-room it was even more difficult. Charlie just kept on eating piece after piece of bread as though to remind Joe of what he'd said about feeding his face, while Joe could eat nothing at all. Then the other boys became aware of the looks Joe was getting from the staff table. Soon even the maids had started a hushed conversation among themselves; all of it, Joe knew, about him.

As soon as breakfast was over, Charlie left the table without speaking and, after a while, Joe drifted along to the day-room and watched the boys set out for school in Carringdon. The snow was quite thick on the ground and snowballs were being thrown. The real battles would take place in the playground lunch-hour when territories would be marked out and teams picked. He and Charlie always managed to be on the same team. Now it was as though they no longer knew each other.

The clock in the hall struck nine. Overhead, there was the hum of a vacuum cleaner. The routine of the Institute was continuing uninterrupted by any concern for him and his problems.

He examined the two rows of books that constituted the Institute's library. With the exception of an old, dog-eared copy of *Tom Sawyer*, few of the books seemed to have been chosen for their entertainment value. And he had read *Tom Sawyer* twice already. But, even so, anything was better than just sitting, staring out of the window.

Soon the magic of the story began to work again and he was at the point where Tom had realised that he was attending his own memorial service when an old van rattled up the drive. His father, wearing a grey suit that needed pressing, got out and vanished from sight before Joe got a good look at his face.

The clock in the hall sounded the hour again;

this time, twelve. He had been lost in the world
of Tom Sawyer since breakfast time.

A maid stuck her head into the room. 'You
are to go to Mr Lawford's study at once,' she
said.

Joe automatically smoothed down his hair.
The last time he'd been to the study had been
to meet the Philipses. Now it was with his
father that he shook hands and with Miss
Carmichael, the social worker, who had
devised the week-end visiting scheme. She
smiled her usual bright smile as Mr Lawford,
from behind his desk, indicated a chair to Joe.

Joe sat and stared at the carpet. He just
could not bring himself to look at his father,
although he was aware of how intently his
father was watching him.

Mr Lawford began to speak in his typically
pompous manner. 'Miss Carmichael and I
have been telling your father how well you've
been doing at school and how much you enjoy
visiting the Philipses. That is true, isn't it? You
do enjoy visiting the Philipses?'

'Yes.' Joe's heart began to pound furiously.
The topic he had not dared discuss with
Charlie was about to be mentioned by no less a
person than Mr Lawford himself.

'How would you like to go and live with them

for a while?'

Joe could manage only a few mumbled words in reply. 'I'd . . .I'd like that a lot.'

'What?'

'I think he said he'd like that a lot,' volunteered Miss Carmichael.

'Like it more than coming to live with me?' His father asked the question in such a way that Joe now found it impossible not to look at him. He was thinner than Joe remembered and his eyes were tired. 'Well, Joe?'

Before Joe could reply, Mr Lawford said, 'I hardly think that is a question that your son should be expected to answer.'

'I don't see why not. After all, you've just asked him how he'd like to go and live with strangers.'

'The Philipses are not strangers.' There was a definite edge to Mr Lawford's voice now. 'In fact Joe has seen a great deal more of them lately than he has of you.'

'I couldn't help that, any more than I could help having to leave him here in the first place. If I'd been able to provide him with a proper home eight years ago, I'd have done so.'

'And are you saying you can provide him with a proper home now?'

'I'm simply saying that I'd like for Joe and

me to get to know each other again. After all, I've paid for his keep here from the day he arrived. . . .'

Mr Lawford was furious that Joe should be told this for the first time. 'Whether a boy is paid for by his relatives or from the Meehan Trust makes no difference to the way he's treated.'

'I'm glad to hear that but, on the other hand, the fact that I have been paying for him does give me the greatest say in what happens to him. He hasn't been taken away from me by a Court Order so if I want him to spend time with me, that's O.K., isn't it?' He addressed the last question to Miss Carmichael, who shot a nervous glance at Mr Lawford before answering.

'Well, yes, within reason,' she said.

'Would it be reasonable for me to take him away for a few days as a kind of birthday treat?'

'Well, there's school to be considered.'

'He'll easily catch up if he's doing as well as you say he is.'

'And the Philipses?' demanded Mr Lawford.

'They will have to wait.'

'In other words, if things don't work out between you and your son, you will then raise no objection to him going to live with the Philipses?' Mr Lawford intended his words to sound sarcastic, but Joe's father chose to take them as a serious remark.

'Exactly,' he said. 'No harm will have been done and Joe and I will have a much more realistic attitude towards each other.'

'A realistic attitude to each other!' Mr Lawford almost choked on the words.

'Well, yes. Isn't that the point to this meeting? To come to decisions? What kind of person would I be to hand over Joe without a moment's consideration?'

'You've had rather more than a moment. I wrote to you weeks ago.'

'The letter arrived on Friday. Blame the post and not me.'

'Blame anyone it seems except you .' Then, as though he suddenly remembered that Joe was still present, Mr Lawford said, 'There is no need for you to remain here. Wait in the day-room.'

Joe's father said, with mock seriousness, 'Best do as you're told before there's an explosion.'

In the corridor outside the study, Joe almost collided with Matron. She looked suspiciously at the grin that Joe could no longer supress.

'And what are you smirking about?'

'My father wants me to go away with him for a while.'

'Oh does he indeed! We'll soon see about that.' She bustled into the study and slammed the door.

Joe ran down the polished corridor, getting up enough speed to slide out through the swing doors that separated the boys' quarters from those of the staff. He was as pleased as when Mrs Philips had told him about the birthday party.

No! No! He was more pleased and all because he had been wrong about his father. His father did care about him; cared enough to have paid for his keep all these years, cared enough to come back and defy the almighty Mr Lawford! If only Charlie were there in the hall with him, Joe was certain he'd be able to find the right words to make things all right between them again.

Miss Carmichael opened the swing doors. 'Well, it seems your father has won the day. You are to go away with him for a week.'

'When?'

'He'll be outside in the car. Pack some warm things. You mustn't think Mr Lawford was being unreasonable. He has a great deal of responsibility and may not always find it easy to communicate. But he does have your interests at heart.'

Joe nodded. He could see the sense of that but he didn't feel like discussing it just then. 'I'd better not keep Dad waiting.'

Six bounds brought him up the stairs and into the dormitory. He took a hold-all from the top of the wardrobe and stuffed a sweater and socks and underwear into it from the wooden chest at the foot of his bed. Then he bounded back down into the hall and out to the car.

'That was quick,' his father said. 'Afraid I might change my mind? Put the hold-all in the back seat. Oh, and do you think you could call me Ned?'

' "Ned"?'

'It's my first name. I don't feel very much like a father yet and if you were to call me "Dad", I might wonder who you were speaking to. Anyway, we could almost pass for brothers. I'm only eighteen years older than you are.'

'That means you're thirty.'

'Only thirty,' said Ned, with a grin.

Beyond Carringdon, a slip road led to the M1. Ned and his son headed north.

Chapter Three

Snow had obscured every detail of the country-side, turning it into a great white space across which the motorway stretched like a giant pencil stroke. Ned stayed in the middle lane, maintaining a steady sixty miles an hour. It was a very different experience to being driven by Mr Philips, whose technique was basically stop-start, slow-fast, so that even the shortest journey would elicit a series of gasps and faint screams from Mrs Philips and, sometimes, even from Joe.

A service station, like a golden oasis in the countryside, flashed past. So too did signs and directions, road numbers and placenames half-remembered from geography lessons.

Then there came a rash of signs for Birmingham that seemed to go on for mile after mile: Birmingham Airport; Birmingham Conference Centre; Birmingham North and Birmingham South. Birmingham this and Birmingham that, Birmingham everywhere until Ned, almost without warning, switched from the centre to the exit lane and down into a tangle of streets through which he drove seemingly without any clear destination in view. Then the confusion of streets became simplified again and, as unexpectedly as they had left it, they were back on the motorway and once more headed north.

'Do you think someone might be following us?' Joe asked.

'Why do you ask that?'

'I just thought that was why you drove around back there. But Mr Lawford doesn't have a car and Miss Carmichael's old Morris Minor could never keep up with us. Anyway, they said it was all right for me to go away with you. They'll have your address if they want to get in touch with you.'

'That's just an accommodation address. That's why I didn't get the letter until Friday.'

'But where do you live?'

'Nowhere permanent or, at least, not yet. That's because of my work. But then you probably don't even know what I do for a living. You probably know nothing at all about me except that my first name is Ned. I suppose I've had so many imaginary conversations with you that I've forgotten we've never had any real ones even when I came to visit you.

'How do you mean "imaginary conversations"?'

'Well, I'd make great plans for the two of us, of how I'd get you back to live with me, and I'd decide to come and tell you, and I'd rehearse it all in my mind. Then at the last moment, something always seemed to go wrong and I'd feel as though I'd let the two of us down. That made it very difficult for me when I saw you, so I'd say nothing.'

'Is that why you'd just get up and leave?'

'Yes.'

'But things are different now, aren't they?'

'They will be so soon as I get a bit of business over and done with.'

'What kind of business?'

'Oh, nothing that you need worry your head about. I want you to treat this break as a holiday. O.K.?'

'O.K.,' Joe said. 'But I still don't understand about you not living anywhere permanently.'

'I'm a musician. I play the guitar.'

'Do you mean at concerts and things?'

'Sometimes, but mainly in pubs and clubs. I made a few records as well, just as part of the backing group.'

'You must be good.'

'Well, let's say that I'm as good as some that made it to the top. It's just taken me a long time to learn how important it is to act quickly, like when I realised that Mr Lawford was proposing to give you to the Philipses.'

'The Philipses wouldn't have taken me if I didn't want to go.' As he mentioned their name, Joe felt a twinge of guilt. He'd just rushed off with Ned as though they deserved no consideration. 'Can I telephone them?'

'Yes, as long as you don't tell them where you are.'

'I don't *know* where we are.'

'Then you won't have to tell them any lies.'

'Was my mother a musician as well?'

'Do you remember your mother?'

'No, not really. It's just that last night I had a dream. There was a woman singing in it. I can remember the words, "The road is long. It slowly winds . . .".'

' "To the house we know so well." ' Ned finished the line. 'She used to sing it to you as a lullaby. I said it was too sad but she said it reminded her of Galway.'

'What's Galway?'

'It's a town in Ireland. She came from there.'

'Had she an accent?'

'One you could cut with a knife.'

'That must be why her voice sounded so strange,' Joe said. 'There was a ship in my dream as well, a big white ship.'

'The only ship she was ever on was the one that brought her to England and I doubt if it was very big or very white. But she loved to tell stories and, by the time she'd finished, her crossing of the Irish Sea had become more exciting than the seven voyages of Sinbad.'

'What did she die of?'

'Pneumonia. But look, do you mind if we don't talk any more about her now? I have a lot on my mind. When things are more settled, we can have a real chat.'

Ned tuned the radio to a station that played country-and-western music. Snow began to fall again. Joe tried to imagine his father playing in a pub. He tried to imagine his mother in Ireland. He tried to imagine Ireland. What did he know about Ireland?

Nothing except what he saw on television: shootings and explosions.

Ninety minutes later, they left the motorway again. This time there was no frantic drive-around. Instead they went directly to a huge shopping-centre on the outskirts of a medium-sized town.

Ned handed Joe a five-pound note. 'There's a take-away over there. Get some hamburgers and whatever you want to drink. I'll have a black coffee with mine. If you find a phone, call the Philipses, but keep it short and no details.'

The take-away was crowded. An Indian family, the women strangely exotic with coats and cardigans over their saris, huddled under a heater and ate quickly out of cardboard boxes. With them was a boy of Joe's age, his brown skin grey with cold. They stared at each other, each wondering where the other had come from, but there was no opportunity to speak. By the time Joe had been served, the family had left.

Next to the take-away was a line of public telephones. Joe got the dialling code for Carringdon from the operator and put money in the box. Mrs Philips answered so quickly that Joe knew she'd been sitting by the telephone waiting for his call. 'Oh Joe, how are you?'

'I'm fine, I'm with my father.'

'So Mr Lawford told us.'

'He's taking me away on a kind of holiday

but we'll be back in plenty of time for the party. Can he come to it if he's still in Carringdon?'

'Yes, of course he can.'

'Oh and could you ring Charlie Morris at the Institute and explain to him that I didn't know I would be going away so quickly? I wish I could explain about Dad.'

The pips began to sound. Joe tried to find more change but the food got in his way. 'I have to go, Mrs Philips. I'll...I'll send you a postcard.'

The pips were replaced by the dialling tone. The conversation was over and Joe hadn't really said anything of any importance.

He went back out into the cold. There was no sign of the van. Then, through a flurry of snow, he saw the lights of a black Fiesta flash. Ned was in the driver's seat.

'Where did you get this car from?' Joe handed Ned a box of food.

'I'd arranged to meet a friend here and do a swop. It has an Irish registration. It'll make us less noticeable when we get there.'

'Get where?'

'To Ireland, of course. That's where my business is. I didn't tell you before in case you let something slip to the Philipses. Also, I wasn't sure how Miss Carmichael would feel about me taking you out of the country.'

'Will we be going to Galway?'

'No. This trip to Ireland has nothing to do with Galway and the past. Now this food is getting cold and, if there's anything I hate, it's a cold hamburger.'

They ate quickly. Then Ned opened his window and tossed the containers into a rubbish bin. 'Right, on we go again. I'm sorry if I keep springing surprises on you but you'll have to trust me. O.K?'

'O.K.,' said Joe, 'but is Ireland safe?'

'The part we're going to is.'

'What about my hold-all?'

'It's safe in the boot. But you won't need it until tomorrow morning.'

Chapter Four

he Fiesta was much more comfortable than the van had been and, when they were back on the motorway, Ned found the same country-and-western radio station and occasionally joined in the singing. The continuous repetitive movement of the windscreen wipers began to hypnotise Joe. He was aware of more road signs: 'Coventry', 'Warwick', 'Wigan', Then the next sign he saw had the word 'Liverpool' on it.

'Not long now,' Ned said. 'You had a good doze for the last few hours.'

'Few hours? What time is it?'

'Coming on for nine-fifteen.'

'We've been driving almost all day?'

'Well, not quite. I pulled into a lay-by and had a bit of shut-eye myself. And of course there were a few hold-ups because of the weather but it looks as though we're right on schedule now.' A sign read, 'To the Car Ferries'. 'We don't even need to go through the city, not that there'd be much to see on an evening like this. But maybe on the way back. Home of the Beatles. Did you ever even hear of the Beatles?'

'Of course I did.'

'They were my idols when I was your age. Who are your idols?'

'I don't know. The Institute doesn't go in much for idols.'

'Apart from that old fellow on the plinth?'

'Do you mean the statue of Sir Joseph?'

'Yes. It's a wonder they didn't carve "Abandon hope all ye who enter here" on it.'

'He affects me that way too; last night, for example, I thought he was going to speak to me but then I remembered it was just a statue.'

'Keep all your thoughts as sensible as that and you'll do fine.'

'Matron says I have too much imagination but when I say nothing at all she calls me "stupid".'

'That's called a "no-win situation". I've been in enough of them to recognise one a mile off.'

The road to the ferry skirted a suburb of

neat houses where the street lights created the illusion of a gap between the roofs and the falling snow. Juggernauts and lorries formed a line outside a great cleared space where one building, a pub, stood as a reminder of the energy and activity that the area had once known.

'I have to get a ticket for you.' Ned pulled up close to an office and ran inside, bowed against the cold. Almost immediately he returned. 'No problems there,' he said.

'Was taking me to Ireland something you only decided on today?'

'Do you mean because I didn't have your ticket already? That mind of yours really is on the go all the time, isn't it, sorting and sifting the evidence?'

'I just like to know things,' Joe said.

'Well, you can't know everything, not all at once, but I suppose you do deserve an answer to that question. Yes, it was a bit of an impulse. When I saw how hostile Mr Lawford was to me this morning, I decided not to take any chances by leaving you in his care. I suppose taking you away was a bit like re-staking my claim to you. And as long as we keep a low profile, everything should be all right. You know what a "low profile" is?'

'Yes, not attracting too much attention.'

An official beckoned the Fiesta forward and looked at their tickets. 'Follow the arrows.'

Ahead, the car decks of the ship were ablaze with lights. Ned drove up the ramp and into a space indicated by a second official. 'So far so good,' Ned said.

He led the way up through the ship and along a carpeted corridor to a lounge. 'Are you hungry?'

Joe shook his head. Now that he was actually on board, he was overwhelmed at the thought of crossing the wind-whipped sea. 'Have you got a map?' he asked.

'A map?'

'Of Ireland and England. I'd like to see where we've been and where we're going.'

'The map'll have to wait. It's in the car,' Ned said. 'But even if it wasn't you could hardly spread it out here without attracting a lot of attention. Good thing you look so Irish or we might have been questioned by the Port Authorities.'

'Irish?' Joe wished there was a looking-glass. 'Do you mean I look like my mother? Oh I'm sorry. I forgot. You don't want to talk about her.'

'It's all right. And yes, you do look like her.'

Ned curled up with the ease of someone used to sleeping on chairs and sofas. More passengers came into the lounge but there was plenty of room so Ned and Joe remained undisturbed in their corner.

The ship's engine began to quiver. An announcement was made over the public address system advising those not intending to sail to go ashore. Ned began to snore quietly, almost matching the rhythm of the ship's machinery. From the bar along the corridor came the sound of laughter and the smell of cigarette smoke.

A further announcement was made; this time by the Captain, welcoming them on board, alerting them to the possibility of rough seas. Joe thought of the Institute, of Sir Joseph's statue, of the dead leaves under the covering of snow, of the patterns on the dormitory ceiling. He hoped the Philipses would pass on his message to Charlie. Poor Charlie! The lights were lowered. People settled down for the crossing. . . .

A blast from the ship's siren woke Joe, but not Ned. Through a porthole he could see people moving around on deck, pointing and exclaiming. The ship must be in sight of land; a land that Joe wanted to see as soon as possible. Joe looked again at Ned. It was surely better to just slip outside than to wake him to ask his permission. All he had to do was keep the low profile.

A woman dressed in angry-looking tweeds made room for him at the rail. 'Come in there now, son,' she said. 'There's nothing in the world to match Ireland seen from the sea. No matter how many times I've seen it before, it still amazes me. Where else would you see a sky like that?'

She pointed to the horizon ablaze with reds and oranges as the sun rose out of the slate-coloured sea.

'Bray Head and Howth Head, guardians of the Bay.' She pointed to the two headlands that enclosed the wide bay and indeed they did look like great, dark creatures keeping watch. 'The Wicklow Mountains.' To the south-east mountains were just visible against the widening strip of daylight. 'Volcanoes some of them were in times past. I don't suppose you were taught that at school?'

'No,' Joe said truthfully.

'And then they'll blame you for not being ready if those same mountains start to belch smoke again, although some people, even this early in the day, have more than a passing resemblance to an active volcano.' She coughed in disgust as a cloud of cigarette smoke crossed her face.

'I'm sorry.' The bearded man next to them threw his offending cigarette down into the water. 'I didn't mean to interrupt the geography lesson.'

'Maybe it's a geography lesson you need at your age.' The tweedy woman abruptly left the rail.

'Oh dear,' the bearded man said, 'I've upset her, but still she will soon be on dry land away from me and cigarettes.'

Howth Head was amazingly close to the ship now, its creature-like darkness strung with yellow lights. A row of buoys indicated a change of direction for the ship.

'The River Liffey itself without a mention of which no arrival in Dublin could occur.' The man imitated the tweedy woman's voice as he pointed to the mouth of the river and a glimpse of bridges and spires rising out of an overhang of smoke. 'Are you familiar with Dublin?'

Joe suddenly realised that if he didn't respond to the man's remarks his silence might rouse the man's curiosity and cause him to ask direct questions. But then he was

totally absolved of the need to speak as a
great blast of wind sent people rushing for
shelter. Joe dodged back into the lounge. But
the bearded man remained at the ship's rail
and, even when the public address system
blared into life and woke Ned, he still stayed
staring out at the water.

'Drivers are requested to join their vehicles
on the car deck as soon as possible.'

Joe was back in his seat before Ned's eyes
were fully open.

'Please do not start your engines until
requested to do so or until the vehicle in front
of you has moved on. Because of the serious
risk of fire, smoking on the car deck is strictly
prohibited.'

Ned stood up and smoothed down his
crumpled clothes. 'Are you O.K.?'

Joe nodded.

'Can you wait for breakfast?'

Joe nodded again.

'You're not very talkative this morning. Are
you sure you're all right?'

'Yes, of course I am.' Joe managed a smile.
Yet in spite of sounding so positive, Joe
wondered if he should tell Ned about the
'geography lesson'. But what was there to tell
of any importance? The tweedy woman would

obviously talk to anyone who would listen. The bearded man had tried to make fun of her to pay her back for commenting on his smoking. And Joe had said only one word, 'No'. That could hardly count as failing to keep a low profile.

In fact by reporting it and making it sound important, he'd have Ned agreeing with Matron about his over-active imagination.

He followed Ned back to the car deck and watched him stick a 'Nothing to Declare' sign on the windscreen. 'Customs,' Ned explained.

The Fiesta was the third car off the ship. The officials paid as little attention to it as had the officials in Liverpool, waving it on into an area of petrol storage-tanks where Ned at once removed the customs-sticker and said, 'Keep an eye out for the N7. That's the road we have to follow.'

Joe didn't need to keep watch for very long. Outside the gates of the docks, a group of signs indicated all the main roads.

Within twenty minutes of leaving the customs shed, they were driving on a fine straight road through gently rolling countryside. The mountains Joe had seen from the ship were visible across the fields to the left. Joe wondered if his mother might have taken this road when she travelled from Galway. Had she sailed on the same ship? Or did ships sail direct to England from Galway? Maybe the map would provide the information.

A flock of crows picked daringly at the surface of the road.

'They must be after dead flies,' said Joe.

'How do you know that?'

'I saw it on television. Although I suppose it's a bit cold for flies.'

'I'd have thought it was a bit cold for crows.' Ned pointed at a squashed heap of feathers. 'Some people never learn. Keep an eye out for Carroll's Bridge.'

The turn-off to Carroll's Bridge was twenty-five miles farther on with a link road that reminded Joe of the connection between the M1 and Carringdon. But, once off the link road, all resemblance to Carringdon ended. The outskirts of the town were defined by thick hedges. Then there was a church as grey as the sky and next to it a school of bright red brick. Then came the bridge that gave the town its name and marked the beginning of the main street.

But Ned ignored the main street and took the road parallel to the river. On the town side of the road, blocks of houses, separated by narrow openings, stood on high ground. Then there was an old stone wall and, opposite the wall, on the river side, a pair of crumbling posts that had once supported gates.

'This must be it.' Ned drove in between the posts and along a winding drive that ended abruptly at a square, ugly house, surrounded by a wild, neglected plantation of trees.

Ned and Joe got out of the car and looked at the house. Several of its windows were broken and blocked with hardboard. The front door hung drunkenly on its hinges.

'Cripes,' said Ned. 'They said not to expect much but I didn't think it'd be this bad. But still we won't be here too long and we can, at least, park the car around the side where it won't be seen from the road.'

The inside of the house was no more welcoming than the exterior. The hall was covered with worn red tiles, and all that remained of the decoration were some damp-looking streaks of green paint.

'The room at the top of the stairs is ours,' Ned said.

The room at the top of the stairs was furnished with a large bed with no bedclothes, a rickety table and two chairs, a cupboard with some saucepans and crockery, a camping-gas cooker and a bottled-gas heater.

'It's colder in here than it is outside.' Ned began to rummage in the cupboard. 'We'll freeze if we don't get that heater lit.' Then he kicked the cupboard in disgust. 'No food and no matches!'

'We can get some in the town,' Joe suggested.

'Oh, yeh? And what about the low profile? You and me driving around with our English accents?'

'You don't have to come,' Joe said. 'I know where the main street is. If I went into a supermarket, I needn't say anything. And you said yourself that I look Irish.'

'So you do, and Carroll's Bridge was chosen because, with all the stud farms and factories in the area, outsiders don't attract too much attention. I did at least remember to get some Irish money.' He gave Joe two bank notes. 'That's ten quid you have there. As well as the matches, get some bread and soup and milk and tea. Oh, and chocolate. What's your favourite kind?'

'Fruit and nut.'

'Mine too. Let's hope we don't end up as a

couple of cases named after it.'

'Can I look at the map when I get back?'

'Sure. And remember, no chats with anyone. I just want to get my business here over and done with without any complications. Then it'll be vroom, vroom back up the N7 and across the sea to Beatle City.'

Chapter Five

Several cars passed Joe. No-one in them even looked at him. Ned's information about strangers not attracting attention seemed to be correct. It was probably even accepted that certain outsiders would stay in the dilapidated house. There was a similar house in Carringdon near the closed railway station. It had once been a hotel. Now it catered for transients but it was not quite as run-down as the house overlooking the river.

As Joe got closer to the bridge, a crowd of children rushed across it towards the red-brick school. Joe watched them, trying to get an idea of their accent.

'Hey, wait for me. . . '

'Maureen Nolan, you're a liar.'

'Better than being a tell-tale. . . '

The words were much slower than those of the woman on the boat, stretching out between the speaker and listener.

'And what do you think you're at?' Joe swung around. A fair-haired boy with the smug expression of a successful bully was standing beside him. With him were two other boys, obviously his toadies; obviously too, from their satchels, on their way to school. 'There's no use trying to look innocent. Rotten, stinking tinker.' He punched Joe in the ribs and pushed him to his companions who spun him back. 'What are you? A rotten, stinking tinker!' He clenched his fist, ready to punch Joe once more.

But Joe dodged and, without considering the consequences, butted the bully in the stomach, catching him off balance.

Then, before the trio could recover, Joe blazed away from them, back down the river road, his mind selecting and rejecting ideas with a speed that matched his feet. He couldn't return to the house. That would attract too much attention to Ned. The blocks of houses on the high ground seemed like a much better escape route. Once he was on the other side of those he'd be safe. The gang would hardly risk being late for school just to chase a stranger.

But, on the other side of the houses, there was flat space criss-crossed with lines of washing, forming a great damp maze.

'The tinkers! The tinkers! The tinkers are stealing the washing!' At first Joe didn't realise that the words were directed at him. Then he saw a woman with bright, red hair advancing towards him. 'Oh, we have you now, me bucko,' she declared.

'But I wasn't. . . '

'Oh, save your breath for the guards. Come on, girls.'

Girls? More women were rushing from the other direction to prevent his escape. The loud whooping of the boys was suddenly very close at hand. Joe dodged under the line of washing closest to him. His foot hit the pole that kept the line upright. The line of clothes swayed. Then it sagged. Then it slumped and the clothes hit the ground with a smack that sent a spray of mud over everyone and everything within range. The women began to scream, but Joe did not dare to attempt an apology. Instead he pushed his way through the washing until, at last, he was clear of the maze and headed for a low wall topped by metal railings.

He squeezed through these and half-ran, half-crawled until he reached a hedge that ended in a tangle of undergrowth. He must surely be far enough away from the town now to be safe. He straightened up and then froze. On the other side of the undergrowth, like three statues, were an old woman, a girl of his own age and the thinnest Alsatian Joe had ever seen. The girl kept the dog under control by the pressure of her hand but her eyes warned that, if she removed her hand, the dog would go for Joe.

'Who are you? What are you doing here?' It was the old woman who spoke. She wore a woollen coat with a shawl around her head and shoulders. Her face was etched with a mass of fine lines that formed junctions around her deep-set eyes and the corners of her mouth.

'I was being chased.' Too late, Joe remembered to try an Irish accent.

'Who by?'

'A crowd of women.' Joe tried the Irish accent now. 'And three fellows I never saw before.'

'Just picked on you, did they?'

'The fellows did but the women thought I was trying to steal their washing.'

'You'll have come from the Barracks so. You don't know what the Barracks is? It's the local name for where the washing is hanging. It used to be a parade ground when the British army was garrisoned here. You don't know that either, do you? In other words, you're a stranger here, although you are hardly here all by yourself. By the sound of you, before you tried tricking us with a different voice, you're from England. And yet you look very like someone I knew long before I came to this place.' She turned to the girl. 'Have you ever seen this lad before, Brigid?'

Brigid shook her head. 'No, never.' The girl had thick brown hair, held back by a twist of ribbon, and pale freckled skin.

'Now why would a group of boys chase a stranger? Tell me that then,' asked the old woman.

'They called me names. They said I was a "dirty, rotten tinker." '

'And you don't know what that means either? Well, maybe they don't have tinkers in England but in Ireland they are the travelling people or itinerants as some refer to them nowadays.'

'Like gypsies?' Joe suggested.

'No, not at all like gypsies. Gypsies come

from far-off places. Tinkers only come from Ireland. We're Irish people. Oh yes, I said "we". Brigid and myself are "tinkers". I'm Maggie MacCarthy. Brigid's last name is O'Donoghue. You'll find all the great Irish names among the travelling people, some of whom lost their land and never got settled again. But what's your name? And what brings you to Carroll's Bridge?' She examined his face carefully again. 'So you're under instructions not to talk? Have you ever been to Galway?' She nodded, satisfied by the effect the word 'Galway' had on Joe. 'But you do know of Galway? Well, I'm from there myself, and it's of someone I once knew there that you remind me. Is it your father you're with for maybe your mother, God rest her, is dead? And I would hazard a guess that you're staying in Oakfield, that old house by the river that Sean of the Mountains looks after, although I'd sooner have a weasel or a stoat to rely on than depend on Sean. When you get back there, tell your father that Maggie MacCarthy from Galway would like to see him on a very important matter. You're to come with him. You'll find me over there.'

She pointed to where the road curved into a shelter of trees and formed a campsite of several caravans and patched tents surrounded by a collection of old cars and spare parts. 'You'd best steer clear of the town for the moment.'

'I'm supposed to do some shopping.' Joe somehow sensed it was all right for him to speak to Maggie. In fact there seemed no point in remaining silent. It was almost as though the old woman could read his mind.

'Brigid will do the shopping for you. She'll show you a safe way back to the house as well, down along the river bank. There'll be no-one there on a day like this.'

The dog made as if to follow Brigid and Joe.

'No, Dingo,' Brigid said. 'Stay with Maggie.'

The Alsatian reluctantly returned to the old woman.

Brigid led Joe to a wider road where a gap in the hedge gave access to a field by the river.

'There's a path that goes all the way into the town,' Brigid said.

'And where does it go if you take the other direction?'

'Up towards the mountains,' Brigid said, 'to where the river rises. But why do you want to know that?'

'Just curious, that's all. What's the river called?'

'The Liffey. It goes all the way to Dublin.'

'To where the boat comes in from England?'

'Yes,' Brigid said.

'Why do you call the dog "Dingo"? A dingo is a wild Australian dog.'

'My brother, Pat, named him that. He saw a picture about Australia once.'

'Does he live at the camp as well?'

'Yes. Along with my four other brothers. There's about twenty of us living there altogether. They are at the horse fair over at Milltown. It was too cold for Maggie to go, so I had to stay with her.'

'Do you not go to school?'

'No, not much. Someone always causes trouble.'

'Like the boys I met?'

'Yes. Some people hate us so much they'd like to drive us as far away as possible from Carroll's Bridge.'

A great white building with a clock tower was visible around the next bend of the river. 'What's that?' asked Joe.

'St Michael's Boarding School for Boys. Did you ever live in a house?'

'Yes, I did.'

'I've often wondered what it'd be like to live in a house. Maggie says it might happen one day. She has the gift of fortune-telling.'

'Do you mean she can tell the future?'

'Lately she's been talking a lot about trouble and strangers.'

'I'm a stranger,' Joe said.

'Maggie didn't treat you like one after she'd got a good look at you. It has something to do with Galway. Still, you'll find out this evening.'

'My father might not agree to come.'

'He'd be foolish not to.'

As the river curved once more, the land on their side began to rise up to form what looked like a cliff to which spindly trees and hawthorn bushes clung.

'Oakfield is just up there so you'd best wait here for me. What am I to buy?'

'Matches, soup, bread, tea, milk, fruit and nut chocolate.' He gave her the Irish money.

'I'll not be long.' Brigid ran off down the path. Joe found a semicircle of bushes that screened him from the wind. Maggie had been right about the river bank being deserted. Then Joe saw a flash of green among the trees on the high ground. For a second he thought it might be a bird. But what bird, apart from a parrot, could be such a bright colour? Joe kept his eye on the same place but there was no sign of further movement. It could have been just a trick of light although there was precious little light of any kind, unlike being on the banks of the Mississippi where Tom Sawyer had lived. But then the River Mississippi was a giant of a river. The River Liffey seemed to have no width at all but it was the first river Joe had actually seen. There didn't seem to be one in Carringdon yet there had to be. Weren't towns always built on rivers?

'Well, you're a fine one to leave alone. I could have been the sergeant of the guards sneaking up on you.' Brigid popped a plastic shopping bag down beside him. 'Maybe you don't know what a sergeant of the guards is? It's what you'd call a police sergeant in England. Now I'm off back to the camp. Don't forget to pass on Maggie's message to your da.'

Maggie's message! How was he going to tell Ned about being chased through the Barracks, much less pass on Maggie's message! Yet he couldn't keep quiet about that as he had about the conversation on the boat. Ned would have to be alerted to the possibility that the woman in the Barracks might go to the police or the guards or whatever they were called.

'Do you know how to get to the camp by the road?'

Joe shook his head.

'Turn left outside the gateway of Oakfield and take the next turn to the left. After you pass the graveyard, turn right. Good luck to you.'

She walked quickly away. Joe lifted the plastic bag and wound his way up the cliff. When he reached the top, he found himself only a few yards from the house. He ran to the front door and pushed it open. Standing at the bottom of the stairs was a small, sharp-featured man as surprised to see Joe as Joe was to see him. Then the look in the man's eyes changed to one of sly calculation. He smiled ingratiatingly. 'Well now, and who have we here?'

The door at the top of the stairs opened and Ned appeared. 'Joe? What's going on down there? Who's with you?'

'Ah, it's only me,' said the man. 'Sean-of-the-Mountains as some call me. I look after this place.'

'You don't do much of a job then.'

'Well, not many have complained lately. But I was given to understand there would be only one of you.'

'The boy has nothing to do with anything. Joe, come on up and let's get this heater working.'

Joe ran past the man and up into the room. Ned slammed the door shut and turned angrily on Joe. 'A snooper, that's all we need.'

'He's the caretaker,' Joe said.

'Don't be stupid. Why would a place like this need a caretaker? And where were you? And don't say "just shopping". I saw you from the window, coming up from the direction of the river. What happened?'

'It wasn't my fault.'

'What wasn't?'

'Some boys chased me and when I tried to get away, a crowd of women thought I was stealing their washing.'

'Their washing?'

'They thought I was a tinker.'

'What are you rabbiting on about?'

'I've told you. They all thought I was a tinker. They were going to hand me over to the police, to the guards.'

Ned suddenly became deathly pale. 'The police?' Then, realising that it might seem as though he was about to hit Joe, he took the plastic bag from him and found the matches.

'Tell me what happened.'

Ned lit the gas heater and, by the time Joe finished his account, the coldness of the room was beginning to diminish.

Ned broke the bar of chocolate in two and threw one part of it to Joe. Still he said nothing.

Finally Joe could stand the silence no longer. 'Will you go and see old Maggie?'

'I don't know. I can't decide anything until this afternoon. In the meantime, we'd better take it easy. The map you were so anxious to look at is there on the table.'

Chapter Six

Being in the room became like being in a space capsule, waiting to return to a real place in time. Ned was lying on the bed, his eyes closed, but Joe doubted if he was asleep. Outside the sky had grown steadily darker as the wind increased, streaking the river with white where it tumbled over a ridge of rocks.

Joe wondered if it was going to snow although he recalled that the wind had been blowing off the land that morning, which would surely mean that the weather in England was being blown away from Ireland. He'd never considered the movement of weather before and wasn't even sure if his conclusions were right. After all, it could be sunny in one place while it was raining only a few miles away. Once he'd driven with the

Philipses through so many changes of weather that Mrs Philipes had said, 'More seasons than miles, if you ask me.' An exaggeration, of course, but it did make the point that no-one could ever make accurate judgements of the weather, or of anything else, it seemed.

So much had happened so quickly; none of it as he had imagined it might be; not that he would find it easy to describe what he had expected except maybe to say that he'd thought it would be warmer and brighter with Ned. Maybe that was because Ned had used the word 'holiday' and that was associated in Joe's mind with the sun and sea; Spain, perhaps, where some of the boys who lived in Carringdon went on holiday, returning to school in September as brown as berries.

He'd bet the boys in St Michael's School went on holidays abroad as well. Farther even than Spain: Miami, the West Indies. They'd have a tan all year round, splashing during the summer term in the natural pool that the weir made in front of the main building.

Had Ned ever been to Spain? Had he ever been anywhere? He looked like a scarecrow slumped there on the bed. He'd lain down as soon as Joe had begun to study the map of the

British Isles. It was a good map with such
detail that Joe had no trouble discovering the
sea routes from Dublin to Liverpool.

Then there was the road from the docks to
Carroll's Bridge, easily traced, as was the
River Liffey rising, as Brigid had said, in the
mountains, meandering past Carroll's Bridge
and then on to Dublin and the sea.

Galway proved to be almost as far west as
one could go before reaching the Atlantic. Joe
traced the route from there to Dublin, softly
speaking the names of the towns and the
villages to himself, trying to picture his
mother passing through them, unless, of
course, she had travelled by train. But
whatever means of transport she had used,
she'd have had no reason to pass through
Carroll's Bridge although Maggie had ended
up there. But what connection could there be
between his mother and that old woman at
the camp?

Ned stirred and sat up as though disturbed
by something. Then he saw Joe and relaxed.
'How are you getting on with the map?' Then
not waiting for an answer he said, 'Cripes, it's
like night time in here.'

'I was wondering if it was going to snow.'

'Don't say that. Snow is the last thing we

need.'

'You managed all right in England.'

'I know my way around there.' Ned was suddenly on the alert again and, moving quickly, flung open the door of the room. There was a faint sound of footsteps on the stairs. 'Our friend downstairs was listening.'

'Maggie says he's like a ferret.'

'A ferret with red hair and big ears is not to be trusted.'

'Maggie said that as well.'

'You've taken a great fancy to this old Maggie.' Ned had closed the door by now and was examining the tins of soup.

'She seemed to know a lot of things, maybe even about the future.'

'Tricks of the trade.' Ned opened a tin of soup and tipped the contents into a saucepan. 'We'd better have something to eat before I go out.'

'Go out where?'

'To make a telephone call.'

'Can I not go with you?'

'No. But, on the other hand, I'm not crazy about leaving you here. If only you hadn't got into trouble in the town this morning.'

'That won't happen again,' Joe said. 'I don't have to go near the Barracks. That road that goes to the camp must divide somewhere and lead to the other end of the town. It's probably even on the map.' He moved the map so what little direct light there was fell on it. 'Yes, look. Here's where we are. You can see there's a back road.'

'You're right.' Ned studied the map in silence. Then he asked, 'Where do you reckon the tinker camp is?'

'Somewhere along here.' Joe indicated the place with his finger.

'So we have a choice of directions in and out of the town?'

'Yes.'

Ned turned the heat up full under the saucepan. 'You could go on a kind of walk-around and meet me back here in, say, half an hour?'

'Yes, only I don't have a watch.'

'Take mine. There's a clock in the car.' Ned poured the hot soup into two mugs. 'Let it cool for a second.' He strapped his watch on Joe's wrist, having to use the very last hole to make it fit. 'You not staying here might actually help. If our friend, the ferret, were to follow you, I could make the call and be back before he'd even know I was gone. If nothing else, it would tell us just how much he was interested in our movements.'

Joe buttered slices of bread. 'Old Maggie knows all about him.'

'Let's leave her right out of things for the moment.' Ned tested the temperature of the soup. 'Which way will you go?'

'Along by the river. That way you can see Sean from the window if he follows me.'

The stairs were almost in complete darkness as Joe descended them; only a trace of light coming through the dirt-dimmed fanlight. He paused at the front door and listened. There was a faint creaking noise as of someone moving around in the room at the end of the hall. Joe cleared his throat and faked a sneeze to let Sean know he was leaving. Then he walked slowly out of the house to the edge of the cliff.

The descent was much easier than the climb had been. Having both hands free meant he could grip at various branches to slow his progress and give Sean a chance to see where he was. But he'd gone only a few yards when he saw the same green object as before, half-screened by an outcrop of bushes.

Then the green object left the bushes and Joe recognised it for what it was: a knitted hat pulled well down over Sean's forehead.

The rest of Sean's clothes were so grey and dirty that they almost provided him with a complete camouflage.

But for Sean to be so far ahead of him on the river bank meant that there was a second person in the downstairs room; a person who could monitor Ned's movements, without Ned even being aware of his existence.

Joe scrambled back up the cliff. Ned had to be warned before he too saw Sean on the river bank and decided it was safe to leave the house. But the Fiesta was already on its way down the drive.

Joe waved and shouted but the car did not slow down and Joe reached the gate-posts just in time to see it turn off in the direction of the mountains and the tinkers' camp.

Almost immediately a second car, dark grey in colour, came from the direction of the town. Joe dodged out of sight among the trees as it passed but got back to the gateway in time to see it head off in the same direction as the Fiesta.

That was too much of a coincidence. It must be following Ned's car. Could its driver be the person they'd heard on the stairs? Had he been in the downstairs room when Joe had left the house? But how could he have got down the drive so quickly? Only minutes had elapsed between Joe spotting Sean and Ned driving off! And where had the grey car been parked?

Joe looked back towards the bridge. There was a cut where a previous bridge might have crossed the river. It would be the ideal place to park a car even if it still didn't explain how the driver had got to it so quickly. But then what explanation was there for Ned driving towards the mountains in order to make a telephone call?

The low profile perhaps? Or, as in the case of the drive through Birmingham, the fear that he was still being followed and needed to put his followers off the scent? But that was a daft notion. Ned couldn't drive forever and the driver of the grey car would know where to come back to if he lost him.

The whole air suddenly seemed to vibrate with questions. But all he could do now was stick to his arrangement with Ned and stay away from Oakfield for half an hour. The river bank was no longer safe with Sean there. That left the back road into the town. It came out, as the map had indicated, at the other end of the main street.

A hotel, its neon sign flickering in the

afternoon gloom, was the first building that Joe saw. Next to it was a telephone box. Ned could have used that without attracting any attention since the main street was empty of people. Indeed the whole town had about it that same feeling as the room in Oakfield of drifting through time; a rectangle of buildings enclosed by streets to prevent it from slipping down towards the river. It would have owed its existence as a garrison to its elevated position and the narrowness of the river at that point.

Joe walked down a side street and came out on one as wide as the main street but with more houses than shops and a market square dominated by a court-house with the date "1846" carved above its windows. Joe glanced at Ned's watch: twenty more minutes to go. He'd walk some more. But suddenly the grey car was coming up from the direction of the river.

Joe ran into the square. The entrance to a derelict coalyard gave him some shelter and at the same time afforded him a view, through its cracked panels, of the side street.

The grey car drove into this street and slowed down. A woman came out of a pub. The driver's window was rolled down. The woman bent down to talk to the driver and there was no mistaking who she was. She was the woman who had accused him of trying to steal the washing.

She stepped away from the car. The grey car drove on, turned left at the main street and went back towards the bridge. The woman headed towards where Joe reckoned the Barracks was.

The street lights came on. Lights appeared in the shops as well. Joe remembered a similar awakening in Carringdon as the school day came to an end. Soon the children would rush home across the bridge. Soon the bully and his friends would be on the loose. There was no point in pussy-footing around and risking another encounter with them. And he had a more important reason for avoiding the gang than just a fear of being pushed around. He'd established a connection between the grey car and the woman from the Barracks. And something more was bobbing up in his mind. It had to do with red hair. The woman's and Sean's were the same deep rust, almost flame colour. And they had very similar eyes. That was why Joe had been so startled to see Sean in Oakfield. Without defining it at the time, he had thought he had come face to face once more with the woman from the Barracks!

He was almost back at the hotel now. Women out shopping looked at him as he ran past but he did not slow down until he was in sight of Oakfield.

Chapter Seven

rom where he stood inside the gate-posts, Joe could see both the house and the road. There was no sign of Sean or of anyone else but Joe knew that that did not mean he was not being watched. But he had no time to worry about such things at present. The main thing was to prevent Ned from driving back up to the house.

Almost to the second, the Fiesta returned from the direction of the mountains. Joe ran towards it, flagging it down. 'You're being followed by a grey car,' he said as he got in beside Ned. 'That wasn't Sean you heard on the stairs. He was already down on the river bank.'

'What are you going on about?'

'There was a second person in the house, spying on us. I heard him when I came downstairs only, like you, I thought it was

Sean.'

'You *heard* the person who was spying on us moving around downstairs?'

'Yes, yes, I did. Please, could we drive on somewhere?'

'All right, but you'd better have some justification for what you've just said.'

'Justification?' Joe stared at Ned in amazement. 'You make it sound as though it's my fault.'

'Or your imagination,' suggested Ned.

'And I suppose I'm imagining those tyre marks as well?' Joe pointed at the churned-up ground by the cut. 'That's where the grey car was parked.'

'No-one could have got from the house to there, no matter how fast he ran, without me seeing him on the road,' Ned said. 'I saw Sean on the river bank too. I was looking out the window. That's how I knew the coast was clear.'

'That's what they wanted you to think and maybe the driver of the car left the house before you did. By the time you got around to the side and started the car, he could easily have got down the drive. He needn't even have used the road. He could have used the bank. I'm sure there's a path just inside the river wall. You'd never have seen him. You didn't even see me when I came back to warn you. Ned, I'm not imagining things! I'm not making it up!'

'I didn't say you were making it up,' Ned said. 'I just think you are connecting things that aren't really connected to make some kind of story out of them.'

Joe's feeling of amazement was replaced by one of anger. 'I'm not a child that has to be humoured,' he said. 'I'm not a complete fool.'

'And what do you mean by that?'

'You said you had to make a telephone call and yet you drove out into the country. How could you know you'd find a telephone out there?'

'Someone could have told me in advance,' Ned said.

'But why would they send you out there when there's a telephone in the town by the hotel? You could have used that telephone without attracting any attention.'

A grin was spreading across Ned's face.

'It's not funny,' Joe protested and then, suddenly, he understood why Ned was grinning. Ned wasn't just humouring him. He was teasing him. He had, in fact, used the telephone by the hotel. He had also studied the map. It had been open on the table when Joe had got back with the shopping.

'The map,' Joe said. 'You studied the map and drove around in a circle to the top of the town.'

'Right.'

'But why did you do that if you weren't afraid you were being followed?'

'It was just a precaution. That's all.'

'But how could you be sure?'

'You'll see for yourself in a moment. But first I need some petrol.' Ned pulled in at a small service station, its forecourt lined with winter-dead plants. The woman who served them was cross at having to come out into the cold and made no attempt to chat. Ned gave her the exact money and drove on, leaving the river far behind, following a road lined with black twisted hedges. Above tall trees, flocks of crows, survivors of hazardous scavenging on the N7, flapped and swooped. Then the hedge-lined road opened out into a great expanse of grass. It was like reaching the ocean.

'This place is called the Curragh,' Ned said. 'It's where the Irish Derby is run.' He pointed to a white rail that curved into the infinity of the afternoon. 'I recognised the name on the map and knew from seeing it on TV how flat it would be and how difficult it would be for a car to follow me without me spotting it.'

'Maybe the driver of the grey car realised that as well. Maybe that's why he drove back to Carroll's Bridge.'

'Maybe too he took the wrong road and realised his mistake. Maybe he was visiting someone. There are half a dozen possible explanations. You say you heard him in the house but you didn't see him? That old house is full of creaks and groans. Every time the wind blows, it sounds as though there's someone moving about. And remember I didn't actually see anyone on the stairs.'

'No, but you believed there was someone there.'

'Yes, until I saw Sean down on the river bank. Oh, I blame myself for what's happening. Taking you away and dumping you in that wreck of a room . . . .'

'I don't mind any of that,' Joe said, 'just as long as you take what I say seriously.'

'You aren't sorry you came to Ireland with me then?'

'No. If only it wasn't so dark and cold.'

'It's dark and cold most places this time of the year,' Ned said. 'And, of course, not really belonging makes it more difficult. Not that I can ever promise you that we'll really belong in the same way as the Philipses do. But you aren't to worry. I promised you we'd have a good long chat later on.'

'Yes, I know you did. But there's more that I haven't told you.'

Ned listened without interrupting to Joe's account of the meeting between the driver of the grey car and the woman from the Barracks.

'What did the driver look like?' he finally asked.

'I couldn't see his face.'

'Well, there's not very much we can do about it now,' Ned decided, 'except be extra careful.'

'You do think you were followed then?'

'Cripes, but you're a tenacious little brat, aren't you?'

'I can't help it,' Joe said. 'I think there's something wrong. I don't even know where we're going to right now. I never know where we're going to.'

'Lots of boys would love the chance to see the Curragh.'

'Yeh, but not on a day like this. It's like the town. It's like the room in Oakfield. . .' Joe looked out at the gloomy greyness.

'It also becomes a part of the past as we drive across it,' Ned said quietly.

'Does that mean we aren't going to go back to Oakfield?'

'Not if things go according to plan.'

'My hold-all is there.'

Ned swore softly under his breath. 'I'd forgotten about that. Still, we'll take care of that later on.'

The grassy flatness of the Curragh yielded to another network of narrow roads. Suddenly the scenery was dominated by a great white statue of the Crucifixion. 'That's the graveyard,' Joe said. 'We're very close to the tinkers' camp.'

'Yes, I know.' Ned was grinning again. 'I passed it on my drive-around.'

'Are we going to see Maggie?'

'I don't imagine I'd get much peace if I said "no", especially since we're so close.'

Brigid and Dingo were nowhere to be seen as Ned and Joe got out of the car, but the door of Maggie's caravan opened at once and the old woman looked out at Ned, taking in every detail of his appearance. Perhaps she had been expecting him and had sent Brigid off to keep an eye out for Sean. Her first words confirmed Joe's conclusions. 'The girl is down by the river so you're quite safe. Come inside. There's tea not long made if you'd like some. No? Then you'd best sit down.'

Ned took the chair by the table. Maggie

lowered herself onto the padded window seat. There was a stool for Joe and, as he sat down, he closed the door.

The caravan was warm and incredibly neat, with the light from an oil-lamp reflected on a collection of brass ornaments, mainly of horses.

'I hear you have a message for me,' Ned said briskly.

'Not so much a message as a warning about the trouble that's coming.'

'Trouble?' Ned wrinkled his forehead as though he had not heard the word before.

'Yes, trouble. The cards when I consult them tell me that certain people are dangerous or bring danger with them. I was alarmed when I first saw Joe this morning but then I noticed the resemblance he had to a family I once knew in Galway and, in particular, to the youngest daughter, Mary.'

Maggie paused as if to give Ned a chance to speak. When he didn't, she continued with her story. 'Mary's people were travellers and she had a sister, Patricia; both fine girls but never contented with their lives. In the winter of '68, the flu carried off both their parents and, a few days after the funeral, the girls themselves disappeared without trace. A few years back, when I was in Clonmel for the races, I spotted Patricia coming out of a shop. If she'd remembered it was a race day, she'd not have gone near the town for fear of meeting someone from her past. And indeed, when she came face to face with me, she was terrified out of her wits. It was only when I approached her in the way I would approach anyone from the settled community, and offered to tell her fortune, that she realised that I wished her no harm and told me what had happened to herself and her sister.

'It seems that they took themselves off to England for fear that they might have husbands picked for them from among the other travelling families and so lose all chance of ever getting off the road. In England Patricia met Owen Murphy, who worked on the buildings, and married him. When they had enough money saved, they came home, bought a bit of land, and Owen continued in the building trade.

'Mary, however, fell in love with an Englishman, who had great plans to see the world. After they married they were forever on the move. Patricia tried to keep in touch but, eventually, her letters were sent back marked "No longer at this address". She assumed that

Mary and her husband had finally gone off abroad and that she might never hear from them again.'

Maggie paused again. This time Ned did speak. 'I'm the Englishman that Mary married. But then you've guessed that already. We never did get to those far-away places. Something always went wrong.'

'Just like when he planned to take me away from the Institute,' Joe thought.

'Finally, Mary was too ashamed to write to Patricia. I suppose she felt stupid after running away from Galway to find a settled life to end up with no place she could call her own.'

'She told you about Galway and her life there then?' Maggie asked.

'Just that her parents were dead.'

'Maybe she was ashamed although she had no need to be ashamed of being a traveller for we are decent people.'

'Decent?' Ned said. 'Living on a site like this?'

'We live here because we've lost our place in the scheme of things. Once the country people relied on us to mend their pots and kettles and cans. That's why we are called "tinkers" because we worked with tin. But we had other skills as well and still do. You'll find no better judge of a horse or a dog than a tinker. And no-one better able to look at the sky and read the weather. Or look at the cards and read the future when she has the gift to do so. If Mary didn't tell you about her travelling life, it was because she feared others might teach you to despise her.'

'No-one could ever have done that.'

'The settled people might have tried all the same. Joe found out this morning what it's like to be a tinker. Think how it is to have to face that every day of your life, even at my age. Oh, on fair days and race days, you'll find plenty who'll want you to tell them the future or, maybe I should say, tell them what they want to hear but will they promise to let me live in peace in my old age? Not at all. Yet that's all I ask. That's what brought me here from Galway, to be close to the last of my relatives, the O'Donoghues. But I don't see much peace for anyone in the cards these days.'

'I don't believe in fortune-telling,' Ned said.

'Not believing in a thing doesn't make it untrue. There is such a thing as a pattern. Time can interrupt a pattern but a pattern can always be resumed when the time is right again.' She looked at Joe. 'You understand that, don't you?'

'Yes, I think I do. When my mother and her

sister went away from Galway, one pattern was broken and a new one started in England. Then, when you met Patricia and heard what had happened to her, the two patterns became one. Now that Ned and I are in Carroll's Bridge and you know what happened to my mother, the pattern continues.'

'That's right. That's right.' Maggie was delighted at Joe's response. 'Some would say it's just a coincidence . . .'

'Others,' Ned declared before Maggie could finish, 'would describe it as nonsense. And I don't want Joe's head filled with mumbo-jumbo about dreams and patterns.'

'What do you know about the Organiser?' Maggie's question had a no-nonsense abruptness to it that caused Ned to respond automatically.

'I've never heard of him.'

'Then let me tell you about him,' Maggie said. 'He's one of the most evil of men, who'd betray anyone, even those who work for him.'

'Well, I don't work for him.'

There was a smell of cooking somewhere in the camp. There were voices too and the sound of returning cars but Maggie and Ned, locked in their verbal and mental battle, were oblivious to anything outside the caravan.

'It's a foolish man who fools himself while trying to fool others,' Maggie said.

'Meaning?'

'Meaning that the truth cannot be ignored.'

'And I suppose you can tell me the truth?'

'The cards can.'

Ned made as if to scoff but Maggie remained unruffled. 'Unless of course you're afraid of what you might hear.'

'I'm not afraid of anything you might tell me.'

'You'll listen to the cards so?'

'All right, but only to prove that they hold no threat as far as I'm concerned.'

Maggie took a pack of greasy yellow cards out of her apron pocket and dealt ten of them face downwards. Then she slowly turned them face upwards. 'It's the same as before: danger and treachery, strangers from across the water, fooling themselves with their own foolish pride.'

Ned pushed his chair back. 'Come on, Joe. We must be off our heads, listening to this nonsense.'

'Call it nonsense if you must.' With one deft move, Maggie swept the ten cards back into the pack. 'Only don't involve Joe with your foolishness. Leave him here with me.'

'What for, since I don't intend to come back

this way?'

'Never say that until you've reached your destination.'

But Ned wasn't listening any longer to Maggie. He'd opened the door of the caravan and pushed Joe out in front of him. A group of tinkers was waiting for them; a tall man, his face as brown as leather, an old tweed hat perched on the back of his head, brought Brigid forward. 'Is this the boy?' he asked.

'Yes,' said Brigid.

'Is this what boy?' Ned demanded.

'The boy that's caused all the trouble for us in town.'

'Leave them be,' Maggie said from the door of her caravan.

The tall man glared at the old woman. 'So you'll take the side of strangers against your own people, will you?'

'The boy is no stranger. He's Mary Ryan's son. He and his father are here at my invite.'

'And will they still be here if the camp is attacked, for we have word that that's what may happen?'

'If the camp is attacked, Joe will be the excuse, not the reason. He's done nothing wrong. He just caught in the middle of it all.'

'That's right,' Joe thought. 'That's exactly

right. I'm caught in the middle.' He looked at the tall man and said, 'I didn't do anything wrong. Brigid knows that too.'

'Brigid never said you'd done wrong.' The tall man suddenly lost his anger and it was replaced by a sense of hopelessness. 'And Maggie, as always, is right.' He looked at Ned. 'You're Mary Ryan's husband so? I'm Mick O'Donoghue. Brigid is my daughter.'

'She did Joe a great favour today and we're grateful to her. But now we have to be on our way.' Ned led Joe through a line of tinkers. It was like running the gauntlet but no-one moved or spoke as they got into the car and drove away.

Ned switched on the radio, an indication that he did not want to talk. He'd gone to Maggie in search of some kind of reassurance that he hadn't found. Now he was almost sulking.

Soon great stretches of pine forest lined one side of the road. On the other side, the land fell steeply down towards the shimmer of the river. In a hollow, there was a cottage with a driveway closed off by a wooden gate.

'That's the place where my appointment is,' Ned said.

'It looks deserted.'

Ned switched off the radio. 'Maybe they don't

go in for a lot of lights in this part of the country. All the same I'd better check it out.'

Further along, a track wound up into the forest. Ned drove along it to a place where it was wide enough to turn the car. 'Stay here,' he said, adjusting the interior light so that it did not come on when he opened the door. He walked quickly back towards the road.

For a few moments, the only sound was of the wind soughing through the trees. Then a bright beam of light was visible down in the valley. But, as suddenly as it had appeared, it seemed to vanish.

Joe rolled down his window and listened. As well as the wind in the trees, he could now distinguish the sound of a car; a car whose headlights had been switched off so that it could approach the cottage unseen by Ned!

Maggie's warning of treachery bounced back into Joe's mind. He got out of the car and ran to the road. He clambered over the gate and half-ran, half-slid down the loose chippings that covered the drive. 'Ned!' he called out. 'Ned, there's a car coming.'

Ned appeared around the gable end of the house as the car drew up at the gate. 'Into the next field!' He hauled Joe over the boundary fence and pushed a flat brown package into his hand. 'Throw this away if you're caught. If not, go back to Maggie and wait there for me.'

'But what about you!'

'I'll be all right. Now just go.'

Joe followed the fence until it ended in a barrier of crossed planks and barbed wire. A splintering of timbers indicated that the wooden gate had been smashed open. The car, its headlights full on, was skidding down the drive. Joe squeezed through the planks into the next field and crouched down out of sight. He could hear Ned's voice quite clearly. 'I was supposed to meet some people here or at least I thought it was here.'

A man said something in reply. It sounded like 'in response to a telephone call. . . '

Powerful flashlights skimmed above the planks and moved across the fields.

The same man as before said something about 'enquiries'. Car doors closed and the vehicle reversed up the drive, scattering even more of the loose chips. At the gate it turned back towards Carroll's Bridge. This time not only were its headlights fully on but a blue light flashed on its roof. Ned had been arrested. Maggie's prediction of trouble and treachery had come true. But Joe had no time to think of such things now. He had to get away from the cottage as quickly as possible in case a policeman had been left on duty there.

He looked towards where he had seen the river. That had to be the same river that flowed close to the camp and past Carroll's Bridge. And to follow the river was surely safer than going back by the road and risking meeting the squad car again.

He picked carefully across the uneven ground, keeping as low down as he could, but soon he was chilled to the bone by the wind blowing down the valley. He could never manage to get back to the camp that evening and yet, if he stayed in the open, he'd die of exposure.

An area of irregular shapes emerged from the darkness. Joe recognised them as machines standing amongst piles of rocks and gravel. He was in a stone quarry.

But there was another shape as well, not of a machine, more like an old railway carriage. Joe opened the door and looked inside. It smelled of tea and stale sandwiches, and was probably used by workers during meal breaks. Well, it would have to shelter him now.

He curled up in a corner, like he had seen Ned do on the ship. The brown package pressed against his skin. He had shoved it inside his

vest without thinking about it. It weighed
almost nothing and yet it was for this that Ned
had crossed the Irish Sea.

The wind howled and groaned through the
quarry. Joe wished he had someone with him,
like Tom Sawyer had had on that island in the
Mississippi, but the nearest he'd ever come to
knowing a Huckleberry Finn was Charlie, and
Charlie was safe indoors at the Meehan
Institute for Boys.

Brigid

Chapter Eight

During the night, the wind dropped and the valley was filled with a thick grey mist through which the lonely cry of a bird seemed to mimic Maggie's words, 'Trouble', 'Trouble', but Joe needed no such reminder of the danger of his situation and the need to get back to the camp as soon as possible. The ground by the river was so soft, however, that it threatened to come over the top of his shoes.

Sheep, like cotton-wool toys, appeared abruptly in front of him and then scampered back into the mist with a terrified kicking of their hind legs. Then a great chorus of barking dogs stretched across the countryside as though alerting the humans to the presence of a stranger. That sound was immediately cancelled out by a thunder of hooves and great snortings of breath as out of nowhere and, seemingly supported by nothing more than the thickness of the mist, a herd of cows passed in front of Joe. Behind them, in close pursuit, a stick-waving man shouted and bellowed and vanished.

Joe felt as though something supernatural had occurred but then supernatural beings hardly used the kind of language that the man with the stick had been yelling, any more than cows of no natural origins would leave behind them so pungent an animal smell.

Joe trudged forward and a denser grey shape began to firm up in the mist and to explain the apparent ability of man and beasts to walk on air. An ancient lichen-covered bridge crossed the river at that point and marked the end of the swampy ground. On the other side, there was a firm path along which he could walk much more quickly and still be concealed by the mist from anyone out working on the land. But then who would be out on the land on such a morning? People would find excuses for staying indoors. Families would be sitting around breakfast tables, wondering what had made the dogs bark. Joe could picture how it would be: gleaming cups and saucers, the smell of bacon.

One of the children, late as usual, would come tumbling downstairs.

'Don't,' Joe said out loud. This was no time to drift off into one of his imaginings. He remembered what Brigid had said about a sergeant of the guards sneaking up on him and, although there seemed to be precious little risk of that happening here, he should still remain alert. If anything should be occupying his mind, it should not be imaginary families, it should be Ned. But what was he to think about Ned? That Ned had been betrayed? That Ned in spite of saying he had never heard of the Organiser was in some kind of trouble that had attracted the attention of the police? That Ned in fact was a crook?

But then was anyone to be trusted? Did Old Maggie actually know anything?

The mist began to thin out, revealing a pattern of empty fields through which the river snaked. The barking of the dogs was replaced by the sound of church bells from St Michael's School. Boys in blazers and flannels came out of the main building and made for the elegant octagonal church. None of them noticed him on the opposite bank. And, if they had, what had he to do with their lives?

Nothing!

A breeze ruffled the surface of the river, bringing with it the smell of wood fires. Joe crossed towards the gap in the hedge and stepped out onto the road.

At once Dingo, followed by a group of variously shaped dogs, charged at him from the campsite.

Joe stood his ground and, with hand outstretched, said, 'Hello, Dingo.'

Dingo cocked his head to one side, recognising Joe, but the other dogs continued to bare their teeth.

Then Brigid came out of the battered caravan next to Maggie's. Her face glowed with relief and she called out, 'It's Joe. He's back.'

Maggie was on her way across the camp within seconds of the announcement, followed by Brigid, who scattered the dogs with a few well-aimed kicks. Behind Brigid came Mick and Nora, Brigid's parents, and the rest of the tinkers.

'Are you all right?' Maggie demanded.

'Yes, kind of.'

'And your father?'

'The police took him away.'

'How did you escape?' asked Mick.

'Ned managed it by letting himself be caught. He said I was to come here to Maggie.'

'Well, better late than never I suppose,' Maggie said.

'Do you know what's going on then?' asked Joe.

'No, not for sure. But this is no place for you right now. The guards were here last night asking questions. Someone reported your movements to them.'

'Do you know anyone in Dublin called "Mulligan"?' Mick asked.

'No.'

'It was his car your father was driving.'

The dogs once more hurled themselves towards the gap in the hedge. 'Sean-of-the-Mountains must be back,' Nora O'Donoghue said. 'He'll have seen Joe walking along by the river.'

'The dogs'll keep him busy for the moment. Like all rats, he's terrified of dogs,' Mick answered. 'And by the time they stop chasin' him, we'll be well away from here, for Maggie is right. This is no place for Joe now. We'll take him to the city with us. He'll pass unnoticed there while Brigid and Pat and myself will make enquiries among the people we know in Dublin as to what's happened to his father.'

'And there's none better than Brigid and Pat for finding out what's going on.' Nora smiled at her daughter and at her son, Pat, a tall, gangling youth with an easy smile. 'Auld Maggie and myself will do a tour of Carroll's Bridge.'

'Aye,' Maggie agreed. 'I've a few regular customers who are in the way of knowing what's going on. Indeed it might be best if the camp was empty for most of the day in case the guards come back. They could search it then to their satisfaction and find no trace of Joe.'

'I have something that Ned gave me.' Joe took out the flat brown package. 'I don't know what it is.'

'We'll bury it among the trees over there.' Maggie turned the package over. 'It'll be at the base of the beech tree close to the set of old tyres. Is there anything else that needs hiding?'

'There's the hold-all in Oakfield. It has the name of the Institute on it.'

'What Institute?' asked Nora.

'Where I usually live.'

'An orphanage?' Nora was shocked.

'More a place for boys who haven't real homes. Ned got permission to take me away for a few days.'

'And he lands you in this kind of mischief! Is he out of his mind?' Nora demanded.

'Leave the boy,' Mick said. 'He's got enough to contend with. Let someone go and fetch the bag while Sean is kept busy with the dogs.'

'There might be someone else in the house, someone who drives a grey car,' warned Joe.

A great silence descended.

'What is it?' Joe asked. 'Do you know who owns the car? I saw it in the town yesterday. The driver was talking to that red-haired woman from the Barracks. She looked very like Sean-of-the-Mountains.'

'It's Sean's sister by the sound of her,' Nora said. 'But I didn't know she was living in the Barracks.'

'To be seen in a place doesn't mean you live in it,' Maggie said thoughtfully. 'But now off with you all.'

Joe and Brigid got into the back of Mick's van and stretched out on a pile of sacks until they were well clear of the camp and Carroll's Bridge. Joe recognised the road that unfolded like a giant roll of ribbon. 'Ned and I drove along this road yesterday. He was trying to believe that he wasn't being followed and all the time they were waiting for him at Oakfield.'

'Well, at least you can rest assured that all traces of you have gone from there by now.' Mick was in the front beside Pat, who did the driving.

'Were you frightened up in the mountains last night?' Brigid asked.

'I suppose so. I didn't have much choice.'

'Choice is a thing few of us have,' Mick said.

'Can Maggie really tell the future?'

Mick laughed. 'I never know for sure what to believe about Maggie.'

Pat said teasingly, 'Ask Brigid there beside you. She's like Maggie's shadow these days. Before long she'll be out herself telling fortunes at fairs and race meetings!'

'You shouldn't make fun of Maggie's gift,' Brigid declared.

'But is it a gift?' Joe persisted.

'Well, let's put it this way,' Mick replied. 'She has eyes as sharp as a hawk and she notices things and remembers things and sees connections. She sees that same ability in you and in Brigid. Your mother had it as well.'

'You knew my mother?'

'Oh yes, indeed, and your aunt as well. Maggie was like a grandmother to them; a bit the way she is to Brigid right now. They say things can be passed on from one generation to another. Maybe you got your gift of understanding things from your mother.'

'All I really remember from her is a lullaby,' Joe said. 'And yet I suppose it had a kind of pattern to it. It had to do with finding somewhere to live.'

'That's a dream most of us have,' Mick said, 'and maybe it'll come true.'

'If I haven't spoiled things,' Joe said. 'From the moment I set out to do the shopping yesterday, I seem to have been in trouble. Unless. . .'

'Unless what?' Brigid asked.

'Unless it was Ned who was expected to go into the town. Everything was supposed to be ready for him in Oakfield but there weren't even matches. If I hadn't been there, Ned would have had to go and buy things. But then the gang would hardly have taken on a grown-up.'

'Why not?' Mick asked. 'There were three of them after all. . .'

'But how could they have known I'd run into the Barracks?'

'They didn't until they saw you do it.'

'And the red-haired woman, Sean's sister, how could she just be there to accuse me of stealing the washing?'

'You're talking about a very small area,' Mick said. 'It only needs one good look-out point to send signals from.'

'The cut!' Joe said. 'Where I think the grey car was parked! I was too busy watching traffic on the road to notice if a car was parked.'

'Maisie, Sean's sister, could actually have been in the car and seen you pass. She got the nod from Sean that you were with Ned and passed it on to the three lads.'

'And from the way Joe described them, they sound like Peter Murphy and the Maguire brothers,' Brigid observed. 'They hate us and are always starting trouble. And Peter's father owns a pub near the market square. Maisie could have come out of there to talk to the driver of the grey car.'

'So everything could have been planned at short notice,' Joe said. 'All they had to do was watch and give signals to each other. But why?'

'Because you're Joe-in-the-Middle just like Maggie said,' Brigid replied. 'You're like the missing piece in a jigsaw and that's why you have to be careful today in the city. Don't trust anyone.'

Chapter Nine

he first city streets of neat houses were interspersed with battered open spaces and small closed industrial estates with groups of sad-eyed men around them, as though they had not yet got used to being unemployed and automatically turned up for work each day.

Next came streets lined with blocks of flats and townhouses that looked as though they had mushroomed overnight.

Then the city changed again with wide streets and tall buildings which gave Joe the feeling that they were there to impress rather than to reassure. Pat pulled in by some trees close to tall, spiked railings.

'Now I want you to listen carefully,' Mick said. 'The city is not too difficult to understand if you remember that the river divides it into the North side and the South side. We're on the South side. Through those railings is a park called St Stephen's Green and it's at the top of Grafton Street. Can you remember that?'

Joe repeated the names and Mick nodded. 'Good. Now at the other end of Grafton Street is Trinity College and the Bank of Ireland. Keep straight ahead and you come to the bridge across the river. That brings you into O'Connell Street. These areas are the busiest in the city. You should have no trouble fitting in with the crowd. You can go to a picture-house later on and meet us back here at five o'clock. We'll be at that building over there close to that church. That'll be the meeting place. O.K.?'

'Yes. O.K.'

'Have you any money?'

'I've the change from the shopping.'

'Off you go so.'

Brigid jumped out of the van with him, wrapping a shawl around her shoulders. 'People would get suspicious if I was in the city and didn't look as though I was begging,' she explained. 'You can cut through St Stephen's Green if you like. It's best if we're not seen together.' She crossed the road and was immediately lost to view behind a line of buses.

Joe walked slowly into the Green. It was beautifully planted with trees and shrubs and, already, the first signs of spring flowers evident in the flower beds. A main path curved around a bandstand into an area dominated by two fountains, whose spouts had been shaped to resemble lilies. People walked briskly over a bridge, spanning a lake crowded with plump ducks and seagulls.

Out of shelters, with windows like portholes, more people could be seen, staring out at the passers-by. They had the same slouch as the workers outside the closed industrial estates.

Two worlds – those who sat and stared; those who walked quickly by.

Joe's slowness of pace left him belonging to neither group. 'Joe-in-the-Middle' again. He increased his speed, heading for the lake.

Beyond it was the main entrance to the park. On the name-plaque in the street opposite were the words 'Grafton Street' in English and in Irish.

As he waited by the crossing, Joe was suddenly aware that a small boy with the creased, amused expression of an old man had fallen into step with him. 'How are ya?' the boy said.

Joe determined to ignore him but then he caught sight of their reflections in the mirrored interior of a shop. No wonder the boy had spoken to him. They both had the same unkempt, unwashed appearance. They both looked like tinkers.

'I haven't seen you around before. My name's Jacko. What's yours?' And then, without waiting for an answer, Jacko grabbed Joe by the arm and dragged him away from Grafton Street.

'Hey, let go. . .'

'Do you want to be caught?'

'Caught?'

Two uniformed figures were scanning the street. Their faces firmed into the hardness of recognition as they sighted Jacko.

'But I didn't do anything. . .' Then Joe realised the foolishness of that observation. Being innocent would not save him from cross-examination. His accent would soon slip and give him away. The connection with Ned would be established. Mr Lawford and Matron would be contacted.

Jacko sensed the change in Joe's attitude. 'Come on,' he said.

A huge van was turning into the main-
stream of traffic. Jacko plunged forward,
taking Joe with him, right into its path. There
was a screeching of brakes and a crunch of
metal as the van hit the vehicle next to it. But
Jacko did not stop. He released his hold on
Joe and ran down a side street and then along
a second street and then along a third street
until he came to a row of tall, dilapidated
houses. He went into the middle one.

Joe followed, stepping across a hall filled
with broken plaster and up a rickety stairs to
a landing where the shattered roof was open
to the sky. From a chimney six pigeons, too
used to city ways to be alarmed by the two
boys, watched cooingly as Joe and Jacko
collapsed in the corner of a room stacked with
fine timber panelling.

'You caused an accident,' Joe said.

'Better than being caught.'

'The guards recognised you.'

'Next time they'll recognise you too.' Jacko
had his breathing under better control now.
'Where do you come from?'

'Nowhere.'

'You're like me so. But I know everything
that goes on in the city so if you want any
information I'm your man.' A squad car

wailed in the distance. 'The accident'll keep them busy for a while but it might be as well if we didn't hang around here. The wreckers'll be back soon for the panelling. Then all the houses'll come down. Do you want to join up with me?'

Joe had no clear idea of where he was in relation to Grafton Street but, more important than the possibility of being lost, was the conviction that Jacko was telling the truth about knowing everything that went on in the city. 'I'll come with you for a while but I have things to do during the afternoon.'

'Things to do,' Jacko mimicked Joe and then pulled a wallet out from under his sweater. He giggled at the look on Joe's face as he spread the contents of the wallet on the ground. 'A good one, eh?' He held up four rectangles. 'Do you know what these are?'

'Credit cards. . .'

'And this?'

'Money.'

'Right. Ten quid for us.' Jacko pushed two five-pound notes down into his shoe. 'And the rest for the. . . ' The small boy stopped abruptly as though just in time preventing himself from saying too much, but there crept into Joe's mind the realisation that the unspoken words might be 'The Organiser'.

'You stole the wallet?'

'Yes, from a dozy old duffer that two of the girls were beggin' from. I snook up behind him and took it out of his back pocket. You should have heard the commotion when he missed it and your two women screamin' blue murder that they never touched the wallet.' Jacko laughed as if at a hugely funny joke.

'But what happened to the two women?'

'Nothing. There was no evidence against them. It'd be different if the wallet was found on them. You don't know much, do you?'

No, thought Joe. But I'm learning. He understood now why Ned had told him to get rid of the package if he was caught. That was evidence that could have been used against them; evidence that Ned was involved in something crooked and that he had involved Joe and Maggie and the tinkers in it as well. But Ned was a grown man whereas Jacko was a child. 'How old are you?' Joe followed Jacko downstairs and watched him throw the empty wallet under the rubble in the hall.

'Old enough to know what to do. Brush some of that dust off you. You look like a snowman.' Jacko slapped at his own clothes and hair. Then, satisfied that he and Joe had shed enough of the white plaster, he stepped quickly back onto the street and down towards a high granite wall topped with railings very similar to those around St Stephen's Green.

'That's Trinity College where the snobs go,' Jacko said. 'It's a university. Did you ever hear of a university?'

'Of course I did,' Joe answered scornfully. Both Mr and Mrs Philips had been to the same university. They had met there and got married as soon as they had jobs. Mick O'Donoghue had mentioned Trinity College as one of the city-centre landmarks so Joe was not too far off the recommended route.

'I suppose you'll be going to one yourself one day?' Jacko tried to be as down-putting as Joe.

'Maybe I will. It hasn't been decided yet.'

Jacko almost stumbled over his own feet when he realised that Joe wasn't just putting on an act. 'And how would you get to a university? Who'd pay for you? How would you know what they were talkin' about?'

'I'd pick it up as I went along just like all the students do. And I'd have passed a few exams at school anyway so it wouldn't all be that unfamiliar.'

'And then I suppose you'd end up shoppin''

in there with all the snobs?' Jacko pointed to a bright shop with huge windows filled with crockery and glass and bedspreads. In letters on the glass were the words 'The Kilkenny Shop'.

'I would if they had anything I wanted to buy.'

'And sit upstairs drinkin' coffee and eating fruit cake?'

'If I was hungry and had the time.'

Four tinker women on the next corner waved boxes at the pedestrians. One of them glared at Jacko. 'Ya treacherous little scut. Who's that you have with you?'

'Me sister.' Jacko stuck out his tongue. The three women shouted after him. Farther along, two tinker children, their thin faces pinched with cold, sat on the pavement with a plastic mug between them. The smallest of the pair said, 'Hey, Jacko. Can we come with you, Jacko? Are you going to the Place?'

Jacko's cocky confidence vanished. 'Keep your mouths shut in front of strangers,' he warned.

'We're sorry, Jacko. We didn't mean. . .'

But Jacko dodged on through the traffic, not waiting to hear the end of the apology. Joe kept up with him but was surprised at how difficult he found it to maintain the speed. 'The Place. . . is that where we're going?'

'That hasn't been decided yet.'

'Who decides it then?'

'Never you mind.' Jacko squeezed through the loose panel of a hoarding that enclosed what had been a carpark. Over one section of it there was a railway supported on three great arches. Jacko pointed to the middle arch. 'Wait there for me.'

'Where are you going?'

'You'll either wait or clear off.'

Joe shrugged and went towards the arch but as soon as he heard the loose panel fall into place, he took off after Jacko. Warning bells were ringing in his head. Something about Jacko suggested that everything was not quite as accidental as it seemed.

Even Jacko's boast of knowing everything that went on, Joe could see now as an invitation to state his troubles, to tell Jacko why he was in the city.

Joe reached the corner of the street just in time to see Jacko go into a shop with the words 'Nolan Vegetables' painted in crooked letters on the name board. The window was filled with sacks of potatoes that made it impossible to catch even a glimpse of what was happening inside. Joe wondered if he dare go any closer but, before he could come to a decision, a hard-faced woman came to the door and looked down the street. Joe swung round and walked back towards the corner, forcing himself to take it at a normal pace but, once away from the street, he ran as he had through the Barracks, not slowing down until he was back at the railway arch.

Almost immediately Jacko came back. 'Did you follow me?'

'You told me not to.'

'Don't try to be smart with me. You could end in real trouble.'

'So could you,' Joe said, 'if I was to tell about the wallet.'

'It'd be your word against mine. Are you hungry?'

The abrupt change of subject took Joe by surprise. 'Yes, I am.'

'There's a great chipper at the top of the next street. Get two pieces of cod and chips. Plenty of salt and vinegar.' Jacko fished a ten-pound note out of his sock.

'I've my own money,' Joe said.

'This money ain't from the wallet if that's what you're worried about. I have that in my shoe.'

'But where did you get this from?'

'It was owed to me.'

Owed? Collected at the vegetable shop? Was it payment for the stolen credit cards? There were gangs that dealt in stolen cards and traveller's cheques, well-organised gangs.

'Are you going to the chipper or not?'

'Why don't you go?'

'It's best if I lie low for a while. What's the matter? Don't you trust me?'

Joe took the bank note from Jacko and went back out onto the street. To get to the fish-and-chip shop, he had to pass the vegetable shop. That was why Jacko had insisted on him going. The woman in the shop wanted to have a look at him.

Joe crossed over as soon as he turned the corner. That way at least the woman couldn't see him until he was actually at the sack-filled window and, even if she came to the door, all she would see was the back of his head.

He avoided looking directly into the shop and there was nothing to indicate that he was being followed. Then all thought of danger and treachery vanished from his mind as the smell of food rolled down over him, causing his mouth to water, reminding him that he had had only a piece of chocolate since yesterday with Ned.

'Are you all right?' The Italian-looking proprietor looked over the plastic counter top.

His daughter paused in the act of plunging fish into a vat of oil. 'He's as pale as a sheet.'

The ground seemed to crumble under Joe's feet like in his dream. A confusion of thoughts and images crowded in on him: the dust in the dilapidated house became like the snow seen from the window of the dormitory, the pigeons on the chimney flew away and became seagulls around the ship's funnel, Maggie called out, 'Treachery, treachery.' Jacko's face loomed largest of all, laughing and laughing and then suddenly frightened and tear-stained. As his forehead touched the warm greasiness of the counter, Joe managed to say, 'I'm all right.'

But the daughter would have none of it. 'You are not all right. Out in weather like this without a coat. You'll sit and eat or you'll not get out of here.'

'But my brother is waiting. He gave me the money.' Joe's Irish accent seemed to be accepted.

'And he will just have to wait a while longer. Now what do you want?'

'Two cod and chips, salt and vinegar.'

'Right.' The proprietor popped a large portion of cod and a mound of chips on a plate. 'That's yours. Your brother's you can take with you. And you need tea to wash it all down.'

Father and daughter watched Joe as he ate, their manner softening into contentment as each mouthful seemed to bring the colour back into his face. 'Good, eh?' the proprietor said when Joe had finished. 'This is for your brother.' He handed Joe a wrapped portion of cod and chips. 'Next time, tell him to do his own messages.'

Joe took the parcel. 'Thanks. . .'

'That's all right. You owe me four pounds.'

Joe touched Jacko's ten-pound note. Then he handed it over. It would cause all kinds of questions if he tried to pay separately.

The daughter said, 'I hope you aren't one of the lost ones,' and Joe knew that she did not mean 'lost' in the sense of not knowing his way through the city.

He hurried past the vegetable shop. The door was closed. From the quick impression he got of the interior, it was deserted. He reached the hoarding and slipped the loose panel back. A curl of newspaper danced across the potholed surface. The middle archway was empty. Jacko was gone.

Several explanations came to Joe. The delay in the chipper had worried Jacko. He'd gone to see what had happened and saw Joe talking to the owners. Maybe he'd been afraid that Joe was explaining where he'd got the money. Maybe the woman in the vegetable shop had come back here to the railway arch and confirmed that he had followed Jacko. Maybe Jacko had just sent him to the chipper so that he could slip away and leave him stranded.

But the warmth of the food in his stomach had brought back Joe's determination of purpose. He'd do as Brigid's father had suggested. Jacko might have seen him get out of the van but he couldn't know about the arrangement to meet at five o'clock. His best bet was to get back to the city centre. And there was no point in wasting the second portion of food.

He ate it as he walked from the railway arches. At the next set of traffic lights, a bus waited for the lights to change. Joe hopped on board and climbed the stairs.

No-one else came up, not even the conductor to collect the fares. So Joe was left undisturbed as he tried to get a fix on where the bus was taking him. There were signs on walls indicating various departments of Trinity College. Then there was a great pillared bank building and, at the end of the next street, a bridge across the river. Then a great wide thoroughfare with statues and trees and seats and cars and pavements crowded with people. 'Last stop,' the conductor yelled. 'O'Connell Street.'

Joe felt like laughing. He'd ended up exactly where he'd wanted to. The conductor ignored Joe's attempt to pay his fare. And Joe saw it as an act of kindness. Maybe the pattern was taking a turn for the better. Maybe Ned wasn't involved in anything dangerous. Or illegal . . . .

Ahead of him was a cinema only slightly less splendid than the bank. A huge sign read, *Together in one programme Star Wars One and Two. Separate programmes 1 p.m. and 7 p.m.'*

Already there was a short queue of children. Joe joined them. The cinema doors opened almost at once. The usher said, 'No pushing there now. Plenty of room for everyone.'

And so there was, for the interior of the

cinema was bigger and more luxurious than Joe could ever have expected, with soft seats, a great chandelier and a huge screen.

The lights dimmed. There were advertisements. Then there was a cartoon in which a cat ate a stick of dynamite and exploded. In the dark, all around Joe, children laughed. A house fell on a mouse. More laughter. Joe laughed too.

For the first time since leaving Carringdon he felt safe, even though that feeling would only last until it was time to meet Brigid and Mick and Pat.

Chapter Ten

Brigid had just left Joe when she noticed Jacko inside the Green. No-one knew Jacko's last name and there were two versions of how he came to be on his own. One was that he had been abandoned by his parents. The other was that he had run away from them because of their drunkenness. But whatever the truth he had a reputation as a survivor and a thief that crooks ten times his age would have envied. And it was clear from his movements now that he was trailing Joe.

Brigid half-ran, half-walked and got to the top of Grafton Street in time to see Joe and Jacko apparently deliberately step in front of the van. When she dared open her eyes again, the street was in total chaos. Drivers were jumping out of cars, gesticulating and shouting at two young guards. Customers and assistants came out of shops, demanding to know what had happened.

But of Joe and Jacko there was no sign.

They must have taken to the side streets and Brigid knew the pattern of these streets. She knew, too, of the dilapidated houses for she, along with others, had often sheltered there from the rain.

But as Brigid reached the corner of that street, she heard the wail of a squad car immediately behind her. She dodged down between two cars, waiting for it to pass. It seemed to take forever, crawling along, then stopping at the end of the street.

Finally Brigid risked being spotted and bobbed up to see what was causing the delay. The squad car was outside the gates to the Dail, where the driver consulted with the policemen guarding the entrance to the Parliament.

Obviously these policemen could provide no information for the car turned and began to cruise slowly back down the street, past Brigid and out of sight.

Brigid ran across the road and into the middle wrecked house. A steady cloud of plaster dust fell down into the hall. A trace of footsteps was by the front door. She had missed the two boys, at most, by a few seconds. They'd have headed down towards the walls of Trinity. And so did she, her sudden appearance close to the Kilkenny Shop startling the begging women and children.

The children Brigid knew well. They were the O'Connors. The women she also knew and knew that they hated her family for refusing to turn into city tinkers. All three of the grown-ups glared at her. One of them said, intending to be heard, 'Well now, would you look at what the wind blew in from the country!'

· To ask about Joe and Jacko would not only be useless, it might rouse suspicions, cause gossip, erect a wall of silence across the city. Better to allay suspicion by offering an explanation as to why she was even in that part of the city. 'There was an accident up at the Green. The guards are chasing someone. The squad car is out.'

The women and children scattered. Brigid looked up. Sean-of-the-Mountains was watching her from the cafeteria of the Kilkenny Shop. He was tidier than she had ever seen him before and he made no attempt to indicate that he had seen her.

So he's in the city too, Brigid thought. He and Jacko are both part of it.

She knew that she had to report back to her father. He'd mentioned the Mulligans in connection with the car that Ned was driving. The Mulligans lived on the North side close to the enormous Phoenix Park. The Thatched Roof pub wouldn't be far from there and that was the most likely place for her father to be.

Mr O'Neill, who ran the Thatched Roof, was well disposed towards the MacCarthys. He had known them in Galway and always said it was due to the fortune that Maggie had told him that he had ended up owning the Thatched Roof. 'I fell on my feet,' he'd say, 'coming to Dublin like Maggie advised and saving the necessary to buy in here when the boss died and his widow felt too grand to run a pub.'

The arrangement had been that the widow got an allowance, a very good allowance, as Mr O'Neill would put it, while he ran the pub and eventually ended up owning it.

Brigid was in the great space of the Smithfield markets now and going towards where the cattle markets themselves had once taken place. Maggie had endless stories about those days of drovers taking herds of cattle by night across the country and of those same herds stampeding in the middle of the city traffic as they were herded towards the quays, to be sent to England on special boats.

'A thousand tales of a thousand tails,' her father would say and, like Maggie, he looked back on those days as the best days of his life. 'The end of an era,' Nora, her mother, would agree. And although Brigid loved to listen to these stories, she often wished there was more positive talk of the future.

Brigid slipped into the kitchen behind the pub. As always, every surface was covered with dirty dishes and pots. Mr O'Neill never seemed to wash up. Brigid sometimes wondered if he just threw everything out and started off with new crockery. It amazed her that anyone would choose to live like this. If she had a house she would keep it so clean and sparkling that anyone could call in at any hour of the day or night and not find a thing to criticise. Settled people seemed to have so little appreciation for things that others would give their eye-teeth for; not that she dared to comment on how Mr O'Neill lived. Settled people could be funny about that sort of thing; all sweet smiles as long as no opinions were expressed.

Her father was sitting in the bar, a glass of stout in his hand. Beside him was a man that Brigid knew to be Mr Mulligan. Mr O'Neill was leaning on the bar; all three were deep in conversation that ceased when they saw Brigid.

'What's up?' Mick O'Donoghue asked. 'Did you find out something?'

'Joe is with Jacko. I tried to follow them but I lost them.'

Mick indicated to Brigid to go back into the kitchen. Then he picked his glass up and indicated to Mr Mulligan to follow him. 'This is my daughter, Brigid.'

Mr Mulligan nodded and smiled. 'Hello, Brigid. Tell us what happened?'

When Brigid had finished, Mr O'Neill sucked in his cheeks. 'The sooner we contact a solicitor the better. I know someone who'll give me the name of one in Carroll's Bridge. And there's Mulligan's car up in the forest. That might not have been found yet. There's not much work done there at this time of year.'

'The most important thing is Joe's safety,' Mr Mulligan said. 'I don't know how I'd face Ned if anything happened to him since it's all my fault.'

'We're wasting time crying over spilt milk,'

Mr O'Neill declared. 'Mick, you and Brigid should be out making more enquiries. Alfie,' he was referring to Mr Mulligan again, 'can do best by waiting at his place in case anyone telephones.'

'Number twelve Joyce Gardens,' Mr Mulligan said. 'In case you want to contact me, I'll write down the telephone number.' He wrote it down twice, then tore the paper in half, giving one piece to Mick and the other to Brigid.

Mick and Brigid left by the side door. 'Where's Pat?' Brigid asked.

'Gone to Tallaght in the van to see if anyone there knows anything.'

'I'll go and try in the Liberties.'

The Liberties was the oldest part of the city, where cleared spaces sometimes provided temporary sites for new arrivals from the country.

'O.K. Meet me back in the kitchen at half-past two. The pub'll be closed then for an hour and we can see how Mr O'Neill got on about Ned and the solicitor.'

'Why does Mr Mulligan say it's all his fault?'

'If we knew that we'd know everything,' Mick said. 'He doesn't trust us completely. And who can blame him with the way others are behaving?'

Brigid cut back through the fruit market. Its busiest part of the day was over now but it was a favourite haunt of Jacko's because of the food he could steal. But there was no sign of him there now. He'd be on the look-out anyway for unwelcome contacts, of which Brigid knew she'd be one. He often seemed to vanish into thin air. His great weakness was that he liked to boast of how clever he was. Often he'd start a conversation to impress others, especially the young ones, with stories of his cleverness. They'd have followed him around like dogs after their master if he let them.

And maybe that was what Brigid should do: create interest. A bragger hates a bragger. What if she was to put on an act that would annoy Jacko and force him out into the open?

At Capel Street Bridge, she saw the two O'Connor children again. They were still begging, holding out the plastic mug. They had obviously decided to steer clear of the Grafton Street area for the present. When they saw Brigid, they began to smirk, certain that they had information that she would love to have herself. But Brigid assumed an air of complete indifference, seeming to notice them only in the most casual way. 'Oh, so this is where you ended up. How's things?'

Fidelma, the older of the two, was clearly impressed by Brigid's manner and couldn't resist a question. 'Where are you going?'

'Oh, just walkin'.'

Maureen, the second O'Connor, said, 'We heard yous were in trouble.'

Brigid smiled wisely. 'Not at all. We're on the pig's back now. Things couldn't be better.'

Both girls rose to the bait now, competing for attention.

'That's not what we heard.'

'We heard something was going on in Carroll's Bridge.'

'Oh, now, you shouldn't believe all you hear,' Brigid said. 'You might as well rely on Jacko to get things right.'

'What's Jacko got to do with it?'

'He thinks that he's the bee's knees but he's only being made a fool of. He's been a great help to us without knowing it. But I'd best be off. That wind comin' in off the sea would freeze you.' Brigid wrapped her shawl more closely around her and walked on. At the top of the hill, in the shadows of St Patrick's Cathedral, old Danny Grade was draining a bottle of wine. 'Hey you, young O'Donoghue, have you any money?'

'Maybe later on, if things go right.'

'If things go right? What things?' Danny tried to get to his feet but Brigid didn't wait to see if he succeeded. By the time she'd reached the Liberties, she'd had four similar conversations. Then she took off her shawl, hid it under her coat and waited in the shelter of a ruined church until it was time for her to return to the pub.

She quite liked this part of the city, with its small shops and poor people. They tended to leave her alone. Maybe they suffered from too much outside interference in their own lives. Or maybe they just didn't want to know. Ask no questions, tell no lies.

The O'Connor children suddenly looked in the doorway at her and hurried off up the hill. Either they were looking for Jacko and had accidentally found her or they were already scouting around for her on Jacko's instructions. Whatever the explanation her plan seemed to be working and would work better once she had reported back to her father and was free to do a bit of tracking all on her own.

She headed for the Phoenix Park, keeping well away from the river until it had to be

crossed by the bridge near the main railway
station. She was half-way across that when
she heard her name being called. 'Hey, you,
Brigid O'Donoghue. Hey, you!'

Jacko was running down from the direction
of the Liberties. But he hadn't a chance of
catching her before she crossed the river and
struck up through the side streets.

As she arrived back at O'Neill's, Mick and
Pat and Mr O'Neill were eating plates of stew
at the less cluttered end of the table. They
made room for her and Mr O'Neill got her
some food.

'I've flushed Jacko out,' Brigid said proudly,
'but Joe wasn't with him. We might still be
able to follow Jacko and discover where Joe is.'

'Can you manage that on your own?' her
father asked.

'I can. Did you find out anything, Pat?'

'Not much,' her brother replied, 'except that
it *is* Sean's sister that Joe saw in the Barracks
in Carroll's Bridge.'

'Oh, I almost forgot. Sean is in Dublin as
well, all dressed up,' Brigid said.

'For a journey maybe?' Mr O'Neill
suggested.

'A journey?' Brigid looked from Mr O'Neill
to her father.

'Aye, he might be planning to be away from Carroll's Bridge for a while.'

Brigid knew at once that there was something she wasn't being told. 'The O'Connor children said something was going to happen at Carroll's Bridge. What do you think it is?'

'We don't know for sure,' Mike said.

'What about Joe's father and the solicitor?'

'Ned is being held for questioning. The guards aren't satisfied with his story,' Mr O'Neill replied. 'It's my guess that he's stalling until he knows that Joe is all right.'

'What'll we do if Joe doesn't meet us at five o'clock?' Pat asked.

'That's worrying me as well,' admitted Mick.

'That's why we have to watch Jacko,' Brigid said. 'If he's taken Joe somewhere and gets the idea that we don't care about him, he might decide he's made a mistake and let Joe go.'

'You make it sound as though Joe was a prisoner.' Pat had intended his remark as a joke but it was at once apparent that he had put into words the thoughts of everyone in the kitchen. Even Brigid, determined as she was to be optimistic, could not deny that a similar

fear had been at the root of her own actions.
'Can Mr Mulligan not help in some way? Can
Pat not drive him to wherever the car is?' she
asked. 'Joe gave us a good idea as to where
Ned left it. If the car was seen driving around
Dublin, it might confuse Jacko and whoever
he's working for.'

'Of course it would,' her father agreed. 'It
would even add to the confusion if our van was
spotted back at the campsite. And to tell you
the truth, I'd be easier in my own mind if I was
back there making sure everything was all
right.'

'Then off you go,' Mr O'Neill said. 'Mulligan
can bring Pat back here to collect Brigid.'

'But I'm supposed to be out scouting,' Brigid
protested.

'You've done more than your share,' Mick
declared. 'Now's the time to stay out of sight
until it's time to meet Joe. Mr Mulligan and
Pat will be back here well before then.'

'Well, all right,' Brigid reluctantly agreed,
hating the idea of a whole afternoon with
nothing to do. Then she thought, I can clean
this place up. I can show Mr O'Neill that so-
called "tinkers" can be as tidy as any settled
person.

Chapter Eleven

oe woke surrounded by music and noise and strange colours. For a moment he couldn't think where he was. Then he saw the word 'Interval' on the screen. He'd slept through most of the film but no-one was paying any attention to him. Instead the audience were rushing to the counter in the foyer or crowding around an usherette selling ice-creams.

Joe looked at Ned's watch. It was almost four o'clock, another hour to go before he was to meet the O'Donoghues. He wished it was time for him to leave. He might fall asleep again if he stayed where he was in such a warm and comfortable place. Maybe an ice-cream would help, or a bar of chocolate. Chocolate had caffeine in it and that was supposed to keep you awake.

He made his way to the sweet counter and waited his turn. He could see the street through the glass doors. The lights were on, giving it a night-time feeling. The passing crowd had the look of people determined to get home with the least possible delay.

He thought of Maggie's cosy caravan. It would be great if he could spend the night there. The sweet sticky smell of popcorn suddenly clogged the air and, to his dismay, Joe felt the same feeling of dizziness as in the fish-and-chip shop. It couldn't be hunger this time. Neither would he get away so easily if he was to collapse in the middle of this crowd. The uniformed usher would surely consider it his duty to get help.

'Hold on,' Joe said to himself. He was next to be served. Once he was away from the smell of the popcorn, he'd be fine. He rummaged in his pocket and a cascade of change thundered onto the terrazzo floor. The usher was impressed by the amount. He stared at Joe. 'Where did you get all this from then?'

'My . . . my father.'

'He must be a very generous man, your father.'

'Yes, he is.' Joe bent to pick up the money closest to him but the feeling of dizziness was suddenly worse and he staggered.

'Glue-sniffing, were you?' The usher nodded to the assistant at the counter. All trading activities stopped as she pressed a button on a telephone. Children stared at Joe as though he was a creature out of the movie. 'And maybe damaging the seats as well,' the usher suggested. 'Show me where you were sitting.'

The manager was coming out of his office. 'It's not glue. It's the smell of the popcorn,' Joe said.

The manager's eyes popped at the word 'popcorn'.

All turned, children, manager, usher and assistant, to look at the popcorn machine. Joe, remembering Ned's advice, seized the moment and was out through the swing doors and into the crowded street.

Tears of rage welled up in his eyes as the fresh air eased his feeling of dizziness. It was so unfair. Ever since he'd left the Institute he'd been treated like a piece of rubbish by almost everyone he'd met. Now he wasn't even sure in which direction he was going.

He eased himself out of the sea of pedestrians and looked around, trying to get his bearings. A sign on the street corner read 'Parnell Square'. Joe had never heard of it but there was a railing around the centre of it and a conglomerate of buses waiting for their crews to work the rush-hour schedule. Joe remembered the conductor who hadn't taken his fare. He looked at the driver and the conductor of the first bus. 'Excuse me, please. Can you tell me where Grafton Street is?'

'Grafton Street?' The conductor lowered his newspaper and looked at Joe. 'What do you want with Grafton Street?'

'I just want to know where it is.'

'It's that way.' The driver was more sympathetic than his colleague. 'Follow the path around there and turn right. That'll bring you into O'Connell Street.'

'Oh yes, I know the way from there.'

In the van, Mick had said something about never having much choice. Joe understood now what he had meant. He had meant that travelling people had no choice about how the settled people treated them. And to complain did no good.

As Joe hurried away a blister on his heel suddenly throbbed into life. But the pain of that was blotted out as Joe stared at a photograph of himself on the front page of an evening paper on a news stand: 'MISSING BOY SOUGHT IN IRELAND'. His hair had

been specially cut for that photograph and he
had grown in the two years since it had been
taken. Even so the cinema staff could easily
recognise him, so could the bus crew and the
Italians. He'd have to get off the main streets
as soon as he crossed the bridge. The crush of
the pavements began to overwhelm him. But
he just had to keep the thought of Brigid and
the van in focus. Once he was across the river,
he'd be all right. Yes, he'd be all right as long
as one of those guards who seemed to be on
every corner didn't pounce on him. They
wouldn't do that if he wasn't so obviously by
himself.

He fell into step with two women, just as
Jacko had with him. But one of the women
became aware of how close Joe was to her. She
at once transferred her handbag to her other
arm and pushed him so that he was forced to
fall out of step and knock against a blind man
begging on the corner of the bridge. 'I'm sorry,'
Joe said and then realised that the blind man
was only one of many beggars appealing for
help from the passing crowd. Jacko's friends
could easily be among them. Joe sprang back,
as from a fire, and reached the pavement's
edge, where the barrier of pedestrians would
give him some degree of cover. At the next

crossing, he didn't wait for the lights but dodged in among the cars and bicycles.

Ahead of him now was the Bank of Ireland, its great pillars floodlit and more impressive than ever. There were more beggars here as well as ticket sellers and young men, blue with cold, preaching a religion.

Joe remained on the edge of the pavement. If he took a side street parallel to Grafton Street, he would eventually be able to cut across to his meeting place with the O'Donoghues.

The side street was narrow and badly lit, jammed with traffic. Life-sized dummies, dressed in the latest fashions, smirked out of a window. He reached what he hoped would be the correct cross street. It too was jammed with traffic. A clock outside a locksmith's told him it was four minutes to five. His timing couldn't be better, or his sense of direction, for now there was only a few yards to go and the lights were in his favour.

He reached the building near the church and waited.

A sharp, cold breeze brought with it a definite touch of rain and, it seemed to Joe, a tang of the mountains. Cyclists wobbled their way around stalled vehicles.

Then the traffic began to move again. Joe looked at his watch. It said four o'clock. It had been almost that time when he'd been in the cinema. Could he have knocked the watch when he'd started to feel dizzy or when he rushed through the glass doors? But the clock on the locksmith's had been going all right. It was just that the O'Donoghues were late, held up by the traffic.

The touch of rain was developing into a steady downpour. Joe tried to shelter in the corner of the building. Traffic seemed to be lessening in volume. A squad car cruised by. Joe moved farther back into the shadows. 'They'll not come now,' a familiar voice said. And Jacko emerged from the curtain of rain.

Joe refused to answer.

'You're waiting for the O'Donoghues, aren't you? The van went back to Carroll's Bridge and Brigid was going around boasting how they'd got rid of a problem. You don't believe me? Listen so.' He beckoned and the two O'Connor children stepped forward. 'Do you recall seeing them this morning? Well, Brigid was following us and she told these two that I'd been a great help to her and her da. In other words, you've been dumped in the city.'

'We seen the van headed for Carroll's

Bridge,' Fidelma said.

'So what about your grand talk now?' Jacko
asked. 'Will you go and see if you can live in
the university?'

'Squad car,' Maureen warned and all three
of them pushed in beside Joe.

'It's not safe here. They're out looking for
someone,' Fidelma declared.

It's probably me, Joe thought. Someone
recognised me from the newspaper. . .

'Where are we going to go?' Maureen asked.

'I don't know about you. But I'm clearing
off,' said Jacko.

'Can we not come with you?' Maureen
pleaded.

'No, not now. Maybe later. Be back here at
ten o'clock. I have things to do. Go on. Clear
off.'

The girls began to whimper but all the same
they went, clinging to each other.

Jacko said to Joe, 'You can come with me if
you like. . . .?'

'I don't need your help,' Joe replied.

'All right, then. Stay and be caught by the
guards!'

'The guards?'

But Jacko was already half-way across the
road towards the railings of St Stephen's

Green. The dark shadow thrown by the tree and the steadily falling rain made him as difficult to see as a wild animal in dark countryside.

Joe ran after him. 'Slow down. My foot hurts.'

But Jacko did not slow down, forcing Joe to grit his teeth against the pain. Then the shoe on his good foot made a squelching sound. It had split down one side, making it even more difficult to maintain any kind of speed.

Jacko led the way into a street where the lights were little more than faint lemon blobs. He squeezed in through some railings and a tangle of hedge. Joe followed and found himself in a garden overgrown with neglected plants, wound like chains around the broken statue of a lion.

Jacko was nowhere to be seen.

A sheet of corrugated iron creaked loosely on a downstairs window. Joe pulled it to one side and climbed into the house. There was a narrow strip of light under the door in front of him and the murmur of voices. Suddenly the door was thrown open. A huge man was silhouetted against the light. When the man spoke, his voice was strangely soft for so big a person. 'You'd best come in,' he said.

Maggie

Chapter Twelve

Fidelma and Maureen looked down the rain-swept street. They had hours to wait before Jacko would return. 'Maybe we could go back to the caravan,' Fidelma said.

The caravan where they lived was in a side street near the quays. With two younger children and so little space, the sisters knew that the later they stayed up the easier it was for their mother. But once they went home, they might not be allowed out again. Their mother had never got used to the city, especially at night. Their father had gone to Belfast that morning to see if he could get into the business of selling TV sets in the Republic. No-one believed he had a chance of succeeding. Competition was tough and local shopkeepers were objecting to losing customers to the travelling people. He was bound to be in a bad temper, siding with his wife in her objections to Fidelma and Maureen leaving the caravan before morning.

'What about the church?' asked Maureen. 'That'll be open until eight o' clock.'

The church that she spoke of was close to where they stood. It was a very famous church where grand weddings often took place. Sometimes the guests would be in a generous mood and give money to beggars. But if too many beggars turned up, they'd get annoyed and threaten to call the guards. But there was no-one around now to challenge the O'Connor girls as they entered the church and squeezed in beside a confessional, relying on its shadow to conceal them.

A woman was following the stations of the cross; her lips moving in prayer, her attention completely fixed on the pictures of the Passion and Death. Apart from her, there were only a few people kneeling before the altar.

The clock above the choir ticked loudly. The swing doors swished open. A figure hurried down the central aisle, looking carefully at the other worshippers. Then, as quickly as it had arrived, the figure left.

'That was Brigid O'Donoghue,' Fidelma

whispered. 'What's brought her back to Dublin?'

'She's lookin' for the English lad, of course. We'd better let Jacko know.'

'But Jacko's gone to the Place. How do we get there?'

'Mollser'll know.' Maureen stood up, startling the praying woman into dropping her rosary. 'She collects the Blind Man from the bridge at six o'clock. We'd best wait a few minutes until Brigid O'Donoghue is well gone from outside.'

Brigid leaned in through the window of Mr Mulligan's car. 'Joe isn't in the church but the O'Connor sisters are hiding in there. I pretended not to see them although I'm sure they saw me. They're bound to go and tell Jacko that I'm back.'

'And that you're looking for Joe,' Pat said from the back seat, 'which makes nonsense of you pretending that we were glad to get rid of him.'

'It'll cause confusion which is no bad thing,' Mr Mulligan said. 'It was no-one's fault that we got delayed in that traffic jam. We have to face the situation as it now exists.'

'And that means following the O'Connors,' said Brigid. 'I'm best doing that by myself on foot. They might notice a car and take to the one-way streets. Wait for me at the corner of Earlsfort Terrace.'

She dodged back down the street and had just taken up a position behind a tree opposite the church when the O'Connors emerged and ran off in the direction of Grafton Street.

The rush hour was over. Few people remained out of doors. In the distance, the bells of the Angelus sounded. Under the portico of the Bank of Ireland, Mollser wound a scarf around her head. It had not been a good day for begging. Cold, damp weather never was. But Mollser was not dependent on the generosity of the Dublin people. She was a second cousin of Sean-of-the-Mountains and had once been a rival of Maggie's in the business of fortune-telling. Most of their clients had preferred Maggie's manner and directness. Her dislike of the O'Donoghues was based on their friendship with Maggie. She would do all she could to harm them. But even if she had never heard of them, she and her closest friend, the Blind Man, would carry out any instruction from the Organiser.

It was Sean-of-the-Mountains who had made her part of the Organiser's network. The Organiser referred to her and the Blind Man as his 'mobile post-office'. There had been plenty of messages passed across the city that day, mostly to do with the boy from England.

'Mollser! Mollser!' The youngest of the O'Connor sisters was tugging at her sleeve.

Mollser glared at her. 'What do you want?'

'We have to get a message to Jacko about the English lad.'

'You can give the message to me.'

'Brigid O'Donoghue is back in Dublin looking for him.'

'Is she by herself?'

'We didn't see anyone with her but she was bone dry so she must have got a lift.'

'You did right to come to me.'

The faint praise delighted the two sisters. 'Can we come to the Place with you?'

For an instant, Mollser almost felt sorry for Fidelma and Maureen but then she remembered that her first loyalty was to the Organiser. 'No, you can't.'

'Well, will you tell Jacko not to forget that he's meeting us at ten o'clock?'

'All right.'

From a shop doorway, Brigid watched Mollser shuffle off towards the bridge. Maureen and Fidelma walked slowly back in the direction they had come. Brigid decided to follow them in case Mollser had told them where to find Jacko. She soon realised that they were headed for the dilapidated house that Jacko and Joe had used earlier in the day.

Brigid got as close as she dared to the front door and listened. She could just make out the girls' voices, Fidelma close to tears, Maureen determined to be brave but unable to hide a tremble in her voice. 'Cowardy custard, cowardy custard.'

'I'm not. I'm not. I just wish Mollser had taken us to the Place so that we could talk to Jacko ourselves.'

That was all Brigid needed to hear. Mollser and the Blind Man would bring her to where Jacko and, probably, Joe were.

Brigid reached Nassau Street. Coming towards her, their heads bowed against the rain, were Mollser and the Blind Man, headed for Merrion Square. Brigid kept them in her sights until they had reached the South side. Then she cut back up to where Pat and Mr Mulligan waited. 'Mollser and the Blind Man are on their way to Jacko.'

Mollser paused under a street lamp. 'What's wrong?' asked the Blind Man.

'I'm not sure. I think we're being followed. But still we'll soon be in out of the rain now!'

'Do you think they've spotted us?' Brigid looked through the windscreen.

'It might be safer to drive round the block,' said Mr Mulligan.

'What if we lose them?' Pat asked.

'That's a chance we'll have to take!'

The next street was darker than the one they had left. Mollser and the Blind Man were in front of them. Mr Mulligan turned off his headlights as, once more, Mollser looked back. Then she led her companion into the overgrown garden.

Chapter Thirteen

he room behind the huge man was crowded with people of all ages, some sitting on wooden boxes, others leaning against the wall. Hissing paraffin lamps threw out heat as well as light, filling the air with the smell of damp clothing.

The man repeated his invitation to Joe, 'Come on in. Or maybe you'd like me to say "please"?' He glanced at the company to make sure that they appreciated the irony of his remark. With instant obedience, everyone laughed and just as instantly stopped.

'They're all afraid of him,' Joe thought. 'That's why they laughed.'

'Why don't you do as I ask?' The man's eyes twinkled. Yet there was an underlying coldness and hardness in his expression. 'After all, Jacko did bring you here.'

'No-one brought me here.'

'You followed him then. That's the same thing, since Jacko is never followed unless he wants to be.'

Jacko was standing by a great armchair that stood in the middle of the room. His eyes were fixed on Joe.

'Why did you choose to follow Jacko?'

'Jacko is a thief and he got me mixed up in it.'

'Dear, oh dear, that's no way to treat a stranger to our city.' The man waved a finger at Jacko and then looked at Joe again. 'You are a stranger to our city?'

'Yes.'

'And if you hadn't been in our city today, where would you have been?'

'At school.'

'School? Did you say school?' An old woman stirred around in a great wet overcoat.

'He said he might be going to the university as well.' Jacko spoke for the first time since entering the room.

'As a student?'

'Yes,' Joe said.

'Well, you're a cool one all right,' the Big Man said, 'talking about schools and universities when your friends have deserted you and your father is missing and the guards want to talk to you about spending stolen ten-pound notes. The fish-and-chip shop owner was very distressed to discover that he'd been so nice to a lad who'd robbed the till of a neighbour. Isn't that so, Mrs Nolan?'

The woman from the vegetable shop was standing inside the door. 'I'd just been to the bank and so the stolen money was in the same sequence of numbers as the ones I had hidden elsewhere.'

'Jacko gave me that ten-pound note. He got it when he left the credit cards with you.'

Jacko flung himself at Joe, his face distorted with rage, but the big man hauled him off with the ease of someone lifting up a terrier. 'Now, now, Jacko. Temper, temper.'

Jacko struggled, furious at his own helplessness. 'I told him not to follow me.'

'Well, he was obviously cleverer than you were on this occasion, more clever in fact than we've given him credit for. It was a good thing Mrs Nolan spotted him. In fact it is a good thing that we have such an efficient network of contacts all over the city, otherwise how would we know what was happening?' He smiled at Joe. 'Word was out about you, Joe. We weren't very sure at first who you were or

why you and your father were here. You
caused us to change some very carefully
arranged plans. That didn't suit us. Now,
thanks to the O'Donoghues' interference,
things have become even more complicated.'

'I don't know what you mean,' Joe said. 'I
didn't do anything wrong.'

'Yes, but who's going to believe that? Or
anything that you say? Have the
O'Donoghues indeed, as the evidence
suggests, abandoned you in the city?'

'They didn't turn up at the meeting place,'
Jacko said.

'And Joe hasn't seen them since they
dropped him at St Stephen's Green this
morning? Oh yes, Joe, you were seen leaving
the van. As I've said word was out. But what's
to be done with you? I imagine it doesn't suit
you to be left on the streets. It doesn't suit us
either. Have a cup of tea.'

Joe shook his head.

'Don't be silly. A nice cup of tea and a nice
meat sandwich.' The man signalled to a thin,
pale woman with dark shadows under her
eyes. She opened a bag and took a Thermos
flask from it.

'I don't want anything,' Joe said.

'You'll offend us if you refuse.'

The woman held a cup out to Joe. He had the choice of accepting it or allowing it to fall. He took the cup.

'Good,' the man said. 'We are reaching an understanding. That might help everyone. . .' The sentence dangled unfinished but Joe knew he was to take it that the 'everyone' somehow included Ned. 'Well, aren't the rest of you hungry?'

Obediently the company crowded around the pale young woman but their eagerness to accept the man's hospitality was false like their laughter.

The man said to Joe, 'Well, now that you've found new friends, why don't you sit down and eat that sandwich Jacko is offering you?'

Jacko nudged Joe over to a corner of the room. Here the two of them sat, Jacko never taking his gaze off Joe, Joe surveying the room, seeing in it a temporary arrangement.

The armchair could be pulled apart and left in the house where it would look like rubbish. The paraffin lamps could be carried away as could the containers from which food and drink was being served. In a matter of minutes, there would be no sign that any meeting of any kind had occurred. If a new place had to be found, there was no shortage of sites and no shortage of people to spread word of the new address.

The Big Man had to be the Organiser.

In St Stephen's Green, Joe had thought of the city as consisting of those who sat and stared and those who went busily along the streets and paths. But now he could see that the division was stronger and more dangerous than that. It was the division between the ordinary people and the people who owed their allegiance to this dark-haired man, seated now on the armchair.

Almost everyone in the room has something to say to him. Some of the information was, to judge from the man's expression, of no importance, just an attempt, as the laughter had been, to please him with a display of loyalty.

But other people were taken more seriously, questioned and given a nod of approval.

Mollser led in the Blind Man.

'You're late,' the Organiser said. 'Is there something wrong?'

'We don't know,' the Blind Man said. 'Mollser has it in her head that we were being watched.'

'I seen this lad earlier.' Mollser stared at

Joe. 'And I seen him in the newspapers as well.'

'The newspapers!' The Organiser straightened up. 'What did it say about him?'

'You know I can't read,' Mollser said.

'Has anyone an evening paper?'

No-one had.

The Organiser spoke directly to Joe. 'Why would there be a photograph of you in the newspapers?'

'I'd have to see the newspaper to answer that.'

'Don't get smart with me. . . ' There was little humour in the Organiser's eyes now. 'Answer the question.'

'I can't until I've seen the newspaper.'

'What's that?' The Blind Man moved to the door. 'There's something going on out there. Someone had better go and see. . .'

Before anyone could move, Sean-of-the-Mountains was amongst them whispering into the Organiser's ear.

The Organiser listened intently. 'There'll be no more business tonight,' he declared.

There was a murmur of protest which the Organiser ignored.

'Be off out of this quick. Jacko. Take Joe and wait until you hear from me. We don't

want you to get into trouble, not with that
new place open.'

Jacko's eyes widened with fright.

The Organiser laughed. 'It might be a good
idea if you told Joe about it. A grand place
with bars in every window where they put
"naughty" boys like you.'

Jacko's eyes widened even more. He
snatched the sandwich and the cup from Joe
and threw them on the ground. Joe ran after
him out into the garden. 'Where are we
going?'

'Somewhere safe.'

'That man is the Organiser, isn't he? What
does he want with me?'

'I don't know. Now come on.'

'Not until you tell me why you're frightened
of him and why you steal for him.'

'He helps me. If it wasn't for him I'd be sent
to that place out in the country. 'Tis a kind of
prison.'

'He couldn't send you there without giving
himself away.'

'Oh yes he could. He's managed to have
plenty locked up.'

'Do you mean like my father?'

'I didn't even know you had a father until it
was mentioned just now.'

Jacko scrambled back out onto the street. A car came screeching around the corner. 'It's the guards again. Come on or we'll be caught.'

He sprinted across the road and the urgency in his voice made Joe follow. Together they jumped a low wall that bordered the canal. A boardwalk across a lock enabled them to reach the other side. The blister on Joe's heel blazed back into life.

'I can't go any further.'

'You have to! Look back there!'

The centre of the road outside the Place was filled with people flapping around in the lights of the car. Some of them made for the canal.

'They'll lead them to us,' Jacko was already on the move again.

Joe kicked off his shoes. The pain of the blister diminished. But the cobbles beneath his stockinged feet had been made dangerously slippery by the rain.

'If we get separated, meet me back at Stephen's Green at ten o'clock. The O'Connors will be there.'

A car was suddenly behind them. Jacko put on another spurt of speed but Joe's body seemed to resist any effort to keep up.

'Joe! Joe! It's us! It's us!'

Joe turned, unable to believe his ears. Then he slipped. The world flipped sideways. He hit the ground. Before he could recover, a familiar voice said, 'Oh Joe, are you all right?'

'Brigid? Where did you come from? I thought you were the guards. Where's Jacko?'

'Gone.' A man helped him up. 'We'd best not hang around here. Get into the car.'

Joe said, 'This is the car that Ned and I came to Dublin in.'

'I know. I loaned it to him.' The man opened the car door and Joe saw his face for the first time. It was the bearded man who had spoken to him on the ship.

Chapter Fourteen

ow did you find me? How did you know where I'd be?'

'Brigid found out,' Mr Mulligan said. 'She followed Mollser and the Blind Man. Then we saw Sean-of-the-Mountains arrive. We were about to force our way in when you and Jacko came rushing out.'

'They're all part of a network,' Joe said. 'The Organiser rules those people like a king.'

'Or a tyrant,' Mr Mulligan said firmly.

Joe's head was beginning to spin again. 'Why didn't you meet me at five o'clock?'

'We got stuck in the traffic,' Brigid said. 'But you didn't really think we'd just dump you, did you?'

'I didn't know what to think. I don't know why anyone is doing anything. I don't know why Mr Mulligan was on the ship. I don't know what's happened to Ned. I feel like a cork that's been thrown into a river and left to bob around.'

'Did Ned tell you anything at all?' Mr Mulligan asked.

'Only that he had business in Ireland and that we were to keep a low profile. I was supposed to treat it as a holiday.' It sounded like a bad joke. 'And now I'm in the evening paper.'

'The people who run the Institute are looking for Ned,' Mr Mulligan explained. 'The woman on the ship, who got cross about my smoking, recognised you so the search was switched to here.'

They were driving along a road of identical neat houses, each with a square garden in front of them. Mr Mulligan drove into an open garage. When he had locked the garage door, he opened a second door that led into the hall of a house that had the same warm feeling as the Philipses' home. A woman as neat as the house came out of the kitchen.

Mr Mulligan said, 'This is my wife, Doreen. And these are Brigid and Pat O'Donoghue and Joe, Ned Mathews's son.'

'Well, well.' Mrs Mulligan shook hands with each of them. 'Ned's son! And what a state he's in. No shoes, soaked to the skin and a flushed face that means he's heading, at the very least, for a cold. You need a good wash and dry clothes. Maybe some of Eamonn's will fit you. Alfie'll show you where the bathroom is. Brigid can give me a hand in the kitchen and Pat can see to the fire in the front room.'

Mr Mulligan took Joe upstairs, opening the bathroom door as he passed it and then going into the room directly across from it.

The room had the same air of neatness as the hall and the kitchen. But it also had the feeling of not having been used for a while. The posters of footballers and pop stars, the transistor radio, the neat line of shoes seemed too neat. Mr Mulligan opened a drawer in the dressing table. 'There are shirts and sweaters here. You'll find jeans in the wardrobe.'

'Who's Eamonn? Will he not mind my wearing his things?'

'Eamonn is our son. He won't mind because has no use for those things at present.'

'Is he away somewhere?'

'Yes,' Mr Mulligan said. 'In a detention centre—thanks to the Organiser.'

'But how did he get Eamonn involved?'

Mr Mulligan sighed. 'Eamonn got into bad company. He started mitching from school, stealing from parked cars. Eventually he was caught and given a second chance. Then a third, then a fourth chance. But the crowd he was in-with kept after him. Finally the judge decided to make an example of him by sending him away. He's due out soon. His mother and I were making all kinds of plans for his future. Suddenly I heard from the people he'd been selling the stolen goods to.'

'Like the woman from the vegetable shop?' suggested Joe.

'Yes. They said that if I collected a package for them on a certain date that they'd let Eamonn alone. But I didn't trust them. I saw it as an attempt to get me permanently involved in their business'.

Mrs Mulligan called from downstairs. 'Are the two of you going to take all night?'

'We'd better not delay,' Mr Mulligan said.

'You still haven't told me what all this has to do with Ned,' replied Joe.

'My job takes me to England occasionally. On one of these trips, shortly after I'd heard from the gang, I met Ned whom I'd known years before. We agreed to keep in touch. As soon as I got word of the date and the place where I had to make the pick-up, the cottage in the mountains, and where I was to make the delivery in England, I asked Ned to do it for me. I left the car where he could collect it. You must have been with him when he did the swap. I hoped that if Ned did the job all right that the Organiser would take him on and leave me alone.'

He looked at Joe.

'Ned is a crook then?'

'No, just desperate to get a new start in life. But I never thought he'd bring you with him. That's why I spoke to you on the boat. I was hoping that I might be wrong, that you might not be Ned's son.'

'Why didn't you speak to Ned?'

'It was bad enough to be on the same ship with him without taking the risk of being seen talking to him. I'd planned to come back by plane after leaving the car but the blizzard closed the airport in Liverpool. I couldn't stay away from work any longer. Anyway, Ned was supposed to be on the previous night's boat.'

'He lost time coming to collect me,' Joe said. 'Maggie would say it was all part of a pattern.'

'A pattern?'

'You meeting Dad. Maggie meeting Patricia. The blizzard closing the airport. Still, I'd better get washed and changed or

Mrs Mulligan will be really cross with us.'

'O.K. I'll leave you to it.'

Joe went into the bathroom and turned on the hot water. Steam covered the glass of the cabinet, turning his reflection into something faint and indistinct like the dream of his mother's lullaby.

Chapter Fifteen

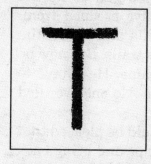he English lad had been caught! That was the terrible thought that pursued Jacko to the quays.

Would the Organiser blame him, desert him, let him be sent to that place down the country?

For a moment Jacko wished he was part of the world of houses and school and universities that Joe talked about so easily. But could the duffers, the settled people, ever be trusted? There had been a woman in Ballsbridge who used to give him food and clothes and a bit of money. Then she had started asking questions about where he lived and who his parents were. He had realised just in time that she was looking for an excuse to lock him up so he stopped going to her house.

The guards were the same, forever trying to trap him. Often Jacko liked to think of the city as the prairie in a film he'd seen with himself as the hero and the guards as the sheriff's men that he always escaped from. The buildings were the hills and rocks, the streets and alleys the dusty trails. But now he was no longer playing a game. He'd have to tell the Organiser the truth. No-one ever lied to the Organiser.

Maybe the Organiser would be pleased that Jacko had managed to escape and bring back the news about Joe.

Yes, that'd be the way he'd do it. He'd go and look for Mollser at the canal. She and the Blind Man were experts at avoiding capture. They'd know how to contact the Organiser.

Joe, Joe, Joe, it was all about Joe now. Joe was suddenly more important to the Organiser than anyone else.

This sudden feeling of jealousy spurred Jacko away from the river where the only sound was that of the rising tide slapping against the quayside.

He passed the O'Connors' caravan parked in the shelter of a disused gasometer. A chink of light was visible through the curtains. Music came from a radio. Had Fidelma and

Maureen come home or were they still waiting for him? He'd never thought of them as being much use until this evening when they had spotted Joe on O'Connell Bridge and followed him to where he was to meet the O'Donoghues.

'I'm a bit like the Organiser myself,' Jacko thought as he climbed up on a mudguard to look into the caravan.

Mrs O'Connor was seated on a chair, a baby asleep in her arms, a slightly older child on a seat next to her. It was like a made-up picture of the kind of happiness Jacko had momentarily longed for on the quayside.

It filled him with anger. He wanted to destroy it before it made him weak.

Like a child raised by wolves who sees humans as his enemies, Jacko banged on the window. The children, startled into wakefulness, began to cry. Mrs O'Connor pulled back the curtain. 'Who's there? What do you want?'

'It's Jacko. Maureen and Fidelma won't be home until late.'

'What do you mean won't be home until late?' Mrs O'Connor struggled with the door lock. It always seemed to stick at the most important moment. By the time she'd got it open Jacko was gone and she had no way that she could leave her two youngest to go after him and demand an explanation. She might as well have been on the side of the loneliest road in Ireland instead of in the middle of the capital city.

The shock that he had given Mrs O'Connor seemed to strengthen Jacko. He knew neither she nor her husband liked him. They'd kept Fidelma and Maureen as far away from him as they could. But Maureen and Fidelma wanted to be taken to the Place. That meant they'd listen to him and not to their parents. Yet despite the feeling of power that it gave him to think this way he was far from pleased when instead of Mollser it was the two little girls who came out of the wrecked garden in response to his call.

'What are you doin' here? You're supposed to be waitin' for me at the Green.'

'And so we were until Brigid turned up looking for Joe,' Fidelma said. 'Did Mollser not give you a message from us?'

'No, she didn't.'

'After we spoke to her we hid in the broken house but Sean turned up there looking for you and the English lad. We got real frightened and followed Sean here but he wouldn't let us come into the house. Then when we saw Pat and Brigid in the car. . .'

'The O'Donoghues were here in a car?'

'Yes, with a man we never saw before driving it. They went up the corner and turned around to come back down to here when you and Joe ran off across the canal.'

'You're sure of this? That the car that drove by here wasn't a garda car?'

'Oh, quite sure. It never even stopped.' Fidelma waited while Jacko thought about what she had told him.

Maureen, however, found the continuing silence unbearable and just had to speak. 'None of it was our fault. The car must have followed Mollser. It was already driving down the road when we got here. We hid in the garden until all the rushin' about was over. Oh, Jacko, what's goin' to happen now?'

'I've important business to attend to. Where did Mollser and the Blind Man go?'

'We don't know.'

'What about Sean?'

'He left with a tall, thin woman. But Jacko, where are you going?'

'I told you, important business. And no, you can't come with me. Meet where we said, at ten o'clock at the Green.'

The vegetable shop was in darkness. Jacko slipped into the yard and drummed on the back door with his knuckles. Mrs Nolan let him in immediately. Sean was hunched gloomily over the fire. He looked even more anxious when he saw that Jacko was alone. 'Where's Joe?'

'The O'Donoghues have him.'

'The O'Donoghues are at the camp. Their van was seen there less than ten minutes ago. I had a telephone call.'

'They're not in the van. They're in a motor car.'

'That means that they're with Mulligan.' Mrs Nolan glared at Sean. 'You were supposed to make sure that the guards found that car in the woods!'

'I couldn't be in two places at the one time.'

'A phone call would have fixed it like you did last night about the cottage.'

'Oh that's right, blab it all out in front of Jacko.'

'Well at least he has more reliable information than you have, breaking up the meeting like that.'

'The story of Joe was spread all over the front page. The guards will have realised by now who Ned is. If Ned talks it'll lead the guards to Oakfield House.'

'So you led them straight to the Place instead.'

'I wasn't followed.'

'Fidelma and Maureen O'Connor followed you.' Jacko couldn't resist a triumphant grin. 'They said you saw them. And it was they who saw the O'Donoghues in the car.'

'You'd better watch what you're saying.'

'Why? Does the truth hurt?' Mrs Nolan asked.

'The truth from a crowd of kids? And if Jacko is so great how come he let Joe get caught?'

'Maybe he couldn't prevent it.'

'That's right,' said Jacko. 'That's why I came straight back here.' Things were working out better than he had dared hope.

'And I suppose you know what we should do next?' Sean shouted.

'No good will come from arguing among ourselves,' Mrs Nolan said. 'And it's obvious what has to be done first. That is to get word to the Organiser and then try to stop the O'Donoghues from interfering. Jacko, what was the last thing you said to Joe?'

'That I'd meet him at the Green near that church at ten o'clock. Fidelma and Maureen will be there as well.'

'Good. Well, you'd best keep that appointment.'

Sean began to protest. 'You surely don't think Joe will turn up there, do you?'

'We have to consider every possibility including the important one of whose side everyone is actually on.'

It was Jacko's turn to protest now. 'You don't mean me, do you?'

'No. I was thinking of the O'Connors.'

'I gave the missus a fright by telling her that Fidelma and Maureen wouldn't be home until late.'

'That could have been a good thing to do. But only time will tell. Now I have an important mission for you to carry out,' Mrs Nolan said.

'A mission?' Jacko tingled with excitement. The cowboy in that western had had a mission to carry out, a dangerous mission.

'I'm going to give you an address on the North side,' Mrs Nolan said.

'The North side? Brigid O'Donoghue was headed there when I last saw her.'

'The Organiser was right to trust you. You're a real bright lad.'

Jacko tingled again. The doubts and fears

he had experienced on the quayside meant nothing. He was about to cross the river like a hero on a white horse.

'The address is the Mulligan house. Keep an eye on it. If you see anyone leave telephone us here.'

'Jacko'll never get across the city in time to be of any use at the Mulligans. I can go and get the car and drive over,' Sean said.

'And what about me?' demanded Jacko. 'What am I going to do?'

'You are going to meet the O'Connors like you arranged,' Sean replied. 'And this time stick to the plan. Just wait until you hear from us. Near the church you said? At ten o'clock?'

Jacko looked to Mrs Nolan for support against Sean. She just shrugged and turned away as though she was no longer involved in what happened. Jacko understood that he had lost a fight that he was barely aware of being involved in. But he also saw that the war was not yet over, only now the enemy seemed to be Sean. Sean would deprive him of any credit for finding out that the O'Donoghues had snatched Joe. But Mrs Nolan knew the truth, knew too that Sean had made a bigger mistake than Jacko had.

Jacko had only been followed by Joe to the vegetable shop. Sean had been followed by the two girls right to the Place.

That was much more serious.

In the western film the members of the posse had fallen out among themselves. The hero had survived by staying calm. Jacko would do the same. His crossing of the river could wait. Instead he'd ride through his own familiar streets.

Hooray for Jacko, King of the Trail!

Chapter Sixteen

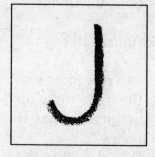

oe and Brigid read the newspaper report together. It was short and to the point, most of the space taken up by the headline 'MISSING BOY SOUGHT IN IRELAND'. 'The search for Joseph Mathews, the missing twelve-year-old English boy, switched to the Republic today following reports that he had been seen on the night ferry from Liverpool.

'Mrs Annie Coughlan, passenger on the same boat, said, "I spoke to a boy who looked very like the boy I saw in the English papers. He seemed to me to be travelling alone."

'The staff at the Meehan Institute for Boys at Carringdon became concerned as to the boy's whereabouts when it was discovered that the address given to them by the boy's father was an accommodation address.

'Mr Lawford, the director of the Institute, said, "Joseph left the Institute, with our permission, for a brief holiday with his father. The possibility that he has been taken out of the country is most worrying." '

'The photo doesn't look much like you,' Brigid said.

'Enough like me for people to recognise me. What about the man in the fish-and-chip shop? Supposing he tells the guards that it was I who gave him stolen money?'

Supper was over. Joe and Brigid were in the front room with Pat and the Mulligans.

'What if the guards realise that Ned is Joe's father?' asked Mrs Mulligan. 'What happens then?'

'We should try and get word to Ned, let him know that Joe is all right,' Mr Mulligan replied. 'Maybe Mr O'Neill's solicitor. . . '

At that moment the doorbell rang. Pat and Brigid half-rose from their chairs.

'Stay where you are, only everybody be quiet. If I have to invite whoever it is in I'll take them straight into the kitchen.' Mrs Mulligan shut the front-room door carefully, making it impossible to hear anything in the hall except the murmur of voices.

Then the door of the room was opened again

and Ned came in.

'Ned. . . ' began Mr Mulligan

But Ned ignored him and the others and spoke directly to Joe. 'Are you all right?'

'Yes, only. . . '

'That package I gave you last night, what did you do with it?'

'I gave it to Maggie.'

'We have to get it back as quickly as possible. . . '

'For God's sake, Ned,' Mr Mulligan said, 'take it easy. How did you get out?'

'Mr O'Neill's solicitor did a very good job. And there was no real charge to answer.'

'But you broke into the cottage,' Joe said.

'No, I walked in. The door was unlocked. All I had to do was to take the package off the table. The owner of the cottage, a Mrs Murphy. . .' Seeing Pat and Brigid react to the name 'Murphy', Ned smiled grimly. 'Oh yes, I thought you'd recognise that name. Her husband owns a pub in a side street near the market square.'

'We think that it was her son who chased Joe. Mr Murphy is always speaking out against the travellers and the camp,' Brigid said.

Ned nodded, 'He's also part and parcel of

whatever the Organiser is up to. I realised
that when his wife turned up at the police
station to get me off the hook. She said there
was nothing missing from the cottage, that
her husband had been up there earlier and
forgot to lock up. The only bit of that that was
true was that he had been at the cottage
earlier in the day. What she didn't say was
that he went there to leave the package for Alf
to pick up. And why was that pick-up made so
complicated? Why was it arranged for you to
stay at Oakfield House and telephone for
directions?'

'I assumed that the Organiser was being
extra careful. Or even that he was playing
some kind of power game,' Mr Mulligan
replied.

'Power game?'

'Letting me know that I had to do exactly as
I was told.'

'But you didn't do as you were told. Why
didn't he get in touch with you when Joe and I
turned up instead of you? Why did the man
who answered the telephone and told me
where the cottage was not question me about
my English accent?'

'Maybe he didn't know who was to make the
pick-up. The Organiser likes to keep things in

separate compartments.'

'All right, but Sean must have known. He'd have been told who to expect, wouldn't he?'

'I suppose so. . . ' Mr Mulligan said.

'The fact that Joe was with me would surely have made him suspicious. Yet no-one tried to cancel the arrangements. Why do you think that was?'

'Maybe no-one could get in touch with the Organiser,' suggested Mrs Mulligan.

'Or maybe it didn't matter who collected the package because the important thing was not who picked up the package but that that person should be arrested with the package on him. Mrs Murphy didn't come to the police station until this afternoon. I think she and her husband went up to the cottage to see if the package was still there or if I'd thrown it away. Maggie spoke about treachery. I don't know if that was just a lucky guess or if she actually knew something. But she was right. A plan had been made to have the Organiser's messenger arrested.'

'Are you saying that the plan was intended to incriminate the Organiser?' asked Brigid.

'Yes, and, of course, the Murphys. '

'And Sean?' Joe asked.

'No,' Ned said. 'I think Sean knew what was

going on. I think he made the call that sent the guards to the cottage.'

'But how could anyone persuade Sean to change sides like that?' asked Joe. 'I saw him at the Place this evening. It was plain that he was one of the Organiser's most trusted followers.'

'Followers?' Ned raised an eyebrow at Joe's choice of word.

'Yes. It was as though the Organiser was a kind of king, or a tyrant.'

'That certainly matches what Maggie said about him. He rules through fear. What were his followers like?'

'Poor people. There was a boy called Jacko who's younger than I am. He has no-one to turn to except the Organiser. Then there was Mollser and the Blind Man. They're all in the same boat.'

'And maybe that boat has sprung a leak. Maybe there are those among his followers who are getting fed up with being bossed around.'

'No-one at the Place showed any sign of that. I think they'd do anything to please him.'

'But there have to be other people involved with the Organiser, people who aren't poor, people who aren't the dregs of society. They might not think that the games the Organiser plays are very funny or that his followers are very reliable. Maybe there's a plot to get rid of the king. Maybe, too, the king is aware of it and that's why he set up this operation in Carroll's Bridge. The town is close enough to Dublin. And yet far away enough for a new organisation to be built up. Who owns Oakfield House?'

'I don't know,' Pat said.

'How long has Sean been there?'

'Maybe a year.'

'And before that?'

'Mainly in Dublin. He used to be a traveller. Now he hates us almost as much as the Murphys do. Maggie says it's because we remind him of his past life.'

'What about the telephone number you were given?' Joe asked. 'Can you not find out who that belongs to?'

'I dialled it as soon as I got out of the police station. A passer-by answered it. It's the number of a public phone box. That was why it was so important that I rang at the exact time yesterday. The man who answered would have to be waiting in the phone box.'

'It sounds to me as though you're saying

that the Organiser's whole world is under threat,' Mr Mulligan said.

'That's exactly what I'm saying. You and I are being used by the Organiser's enemies to try and make his plans for Carroll's Bridge backfire. Maybe Sean is fed up being stuck in Oakfield House. It's hardly better than the camp. Maybe he thinks he'll get some kind of promotion if he changes sides. He must have been made some kind of promise to take the chance he's taken.'

'He was in Dublin all dressed up,' Brigid said

'To impress his new friends no doubt.'

'And to maybe see what had happened to Joe.'

'You were in Dublin all day, Joe?'

'Yes. And now there's this.' Joe handed Ned the newspaper.

'Cripes,' Ned said. 'Once the guards who questioned me see this we'll really be up the spout. Mr Lawford will have a field day.'

'Are you sending me back to the Institute then?'

'This may be hard for you to understand but when I was caught last night and had to leave you alone on the mountain I realised that I had just been fooling myself into thinking there was nothing wrong in taking Alf's place. I knew in my heart that I was involved in something dodgy. You don't get paid that kind of money for collecting a package from an isolated cottage if everything is on the up-and-up.'

'The money came from me,' Mr Mulligan said, 'and not the Organiser. I knew you were hard up and that it would tempt you. But I never figured on Joe being involved. I was thinking of my own son's future.'

'And we both went through a kind of madness,' Ned said. 'Now we have to try and put an end to it. The Murphys and the Organiser are bound to know by now that I've been let go. That could only mean that the package wasn't found on me. Sean and whoever he's working for will realise the same thing. How long will it be before they guess that Joe knows where it is?'

'What are we going to do?' Joe asked.

'Find the package and see what's in it. Then get in touch with the solicitor again and ask his advice. But before I talk to him I want you safely out of Ireland,' Ned replied.

'That might be easier said than done,' Mr Mulligan said. 'The ports and the airport will be on the alert.'

'And Mr Lawford will find a way to prevent you visiting me again. The Philipses might not want me when they hear what's happened. I'm half-tinker. I'm Joe-in-the-Middle.'

'But I've got nowhere to take you. We're worse off than we were when we left Liverpool.'

'No, we aren't,' Joe said. 'We know each other now.'

'Do we really?'

'Oh yes. We've been through a lot. If there's more to go through I want to help.'

Mrs Mulligan gave Joe a hug. 'Well, you can't say fairer than that. Alf and I will do what we can to help too.'

'O.K.,' Ned said, 'but we'll have to move carefully.'

'This house is probably being watched,' Mr Mulligan said, 'by one of the Organiser's lot. We can't just all get into the car and head off for Carroll's Bridge.'

'We really need two cars in order to create a diversion,' Ned said.

'Mr O'Neill has a car,' Bridget said.

'That's true. And he'd lend it to me,' Mr Mulligan said, 'but what about the diversion?'

'I'm nearly the same height as Joe,' Brigid

said. 'If I were to put on his sweater and sit in the back of your car with Joe's da driving it might look as though Joe had been taken away from here. We could go in the direction of the docks. They might think we were making for the night boat back to Liverpool. Joe could go to Carroll's Bridge with Pat and Mr Mulligan. I know that Maggie'll only give the package to Joe. If Mr Mulligan dropped him near the bridge Joe could easily get back to the camp without being seen. Pat and Mr Mulligan might be able to find out if there's anything happening in the town.'

'And how do we all meet up later on?' Ned asked.

'There's a quarry by the river with a kind of workmen's hut in it,' Joe said. 'There must be a road to it that doesn't go through Carroll's Bridge.'

'Yes, there is, from the other side of the mountain. I know the way well,' Brigid said.

'I'll go and get you the sweater,' said Joe.

With her hair pulled back off her face and tucked into the sweater, Brigid looked quite different. She sat on the back seat with her face turned away from the window. Alf handed Ned the car keys. 'Good luck. Still mates?'

'Of course we are.' Then Ned looked at Joe. 'I'm proud of you.'

'I'm proud of you too,' Joe replied, 'for trying to make things right.'

'You'd better go back into the hall.'

'Better again upstairs,' Mrs Mulligan said. 'We'll be able to look out without being seen.'

Mr Mulligan opened the garage door. Ned revved the engine. There was a cloud of fumes as he drove out into Joyce Gardens.

Second's later Sean emerged from the shadows and hurried down towards the main road.

'He's never going to follow them on foot.'

Mrs Mulligan's query was answered almost at once. The lights of a car parked under a broken street lamp came on. It was the same grey car as Joe had seen in Carroll's Bridge.

'Will you be all right here, Mrs Mulligan?' Joe asked. 'What if the Organiser sends someone around here while you're on your own?'

'I won't answer the door.'

'There won't be any callers,' Mr Mulligan said. 'The Organiser knows by now that someone has doubled-crossed him. He'll wait until he has a good idea who that is. Then he'll try and pounce. He'll know too that Sean is no longer to be trusted. Now I'm going to slip over to Mr O'Neill. Pat and Joe, you follow me in about five minutes.'

Chapter Seventeen

he rain had turned the suburbs into a glistening carousel of dripping trees and shining pavements. All the roads looked the same with identical houses. Then came shops filled with well-dressed people. There were pubs as well and restaurants and smart clean petrol stations.

Then the streets became dark with few lights in the buildings. There were almost no pedestrians to be seen.

'St Stephen's Green straight ahead,' Mr Mulligan said.

Joe stared in amazement at the blackness surrounded by metal railings. The fountains would be turned off. The shelters would be empty. Ducks would be asleep, their heads tucked under their wings.

'We'll be passing the church in a few

seconds,' Mr Mulligan said. 'I don't dare slow down but you have a quick look and see if Jacko did turn up. If he's there it'll mean that your father was right, that the Organiser still wants to get his hands on you.'

Joe swivelled around in his seat. 'There's definitely someone there. Maybe more than one. It could be the O'Connor girls.'

A familiar figure ran across the road.

'That's Jacko arriving now. Oh, Mr Mulligan, could you stop and let me have a word with him? He just might tell me something. I'll take Pat with me.'

Jacko popped his head out as soon as he heard footsteps. 'You're supposed to be by yourself. The O'Donoghues are all against us.'

'No, they're not. They'll help you if you'll let them.'

'How? By getting me into trouble. The Organiser and Sean know everything that's going on.'

'Do they know that you arranged to meet Joe here?' Pat glanced down the street. Two cars were coming into sight, one behind the other, both moving at the same speed as though they were at the head of an invisible procession. 'Was someone to pick you up?'

'No, I was to bring Joe to the veg. . . .'

Jacko's voice faltered as he watched the progress of the cars. 'What's goin' on?'

'I think the guards have been told where to find you.'

'The guards? Who did that? They'll lock me up!'

'Don't run,' Joe said. 'You've no reason to run.'

But Jacko had already broken cover and was headed for the two cars.

'He's going in the wrong direction.'

'No. The cars will have to turn around to follow him. It's a one-way system so they'll have to drive into on-coming traffic. He has a better chance of getting away,' Pat said. 'But we'd better get back to Mr Mulligan.'

'What about us?' Fidelma and Maureen were right behind them.

'We can't leave them here. We just can't,' Joe said.

The two little girls caught up with them.

'What happened? Who are these?' Mr Mulligan looked anxiously out of the car.

'Fidelma and Maureen O'Connor. The guards were told that we were meeting near the church. We think Jacko got away.'

'More of Sean's dirty work,' said Mr Mulligan. 'Where do these young ones live?'

'Down off the quays,' Pat said.

'Mammy'll be real cross if she knew we were with Jacko.' Maureen began to cry. So did Fidelma.

'Well, she has to know. What good did you think it'd do you to run around with him anyway?'

'He was going to take us to the Place.'

'Yes, and turn you into a couple of thieves.'

A Guinness ship, its gangway bright with lights, bobbed up and down on the full tide. Trucks and cars bounced on the uneven road. It was as though they had been sheltering until the rain was over and now felt that it was safe to come back out.

The door of the O'Connors' caravan was open, the girls' parents talking to two men.

'Them's our uncles,' Maureen said. 'They went to Belfast with Da.'

As Mr Mulligan slowed down, O'Connor yanked the car door open. 'What the blazes are you doin' with my girls?'

'Returning them safely to you from the clutches of young Jacko.'

'They were with Jacko?' Mrs O'Connor came forward. 'But we thought it was the O'Donoghues who were leading them astray. That's Pat O'Donoghue there with you, isn't it?'

'Yes. But who warned you against the O'Donoghues?'

'Mollser and the Blind Man. They came around here after Jacko frightened the life out of me by banging on the window.'

'Sean-of-the-Mountains put them up to it,' Pat said.

'If you'll take my advice you'll keep those girls of yours indoors for a few days,' Mr Mulligan said.

'We've always done our best to avoid Mollser and that lot. Even when they've come around offering odd jobs to John-Jo.'

'Well, let them get your daughters into their clutches and it won't be a question of them offering your husband work. It'll be a question of making him do it.'

Mr Mulligan drove through the city with great skill. Traffic lights turned green as soon as they approached them. Within minutes they were back on the dual carriageway.

The countryside was as dark as the interior of St Stephen's Green with an occasional square of light indicating a house. Then came the turn off to Carroll's Bridge, the church and the school.

'Drop me here,' Joe said. 'I know how to get to the camp through the Barracks. No-one will expect me to go that way.'

The moon appeared briefly from behind rain clouds, silvering roofs as Joe ran up the incline into the Barracks. The lines were still heavy with washing. He reached the railings and was about to slip through them when he heard a cheer as though a goal had been scored at a football match. There was another burst of sound, of voices raised.

It's a public meeting of some kind, Joe realised. But a meeting about what?

It could be of the utmost importance for him to find out.

Joe crossed the main street and looked down the side street where the Murphys' pub was. The market square at the other end was thronged with people. The red-haired woman was speaking, looking down on the crowd.

'I tell you that what was said here tonight is true. The tinkers bring nothing but filth and crime and trouble. I've lived in the Barracks only a short time but I've found, like every other woman in it, that you can't put out as much as a tea-towel without it being whipped off the line. And what about Peter Murphy? Where are you, Peter? Come on up here.'

The boy who had attacked Joe appeared

beside the red-haired woman.

'This poor child was set-on on his way to school and an attempt made to rob him. Even now while we are here, trying to defend our town, our houses might be being broken into.'

'In that case maybe we'd be better off at home,' a jolly-sounding man yelled.

'It's no joke,' the red-haired woman yelled back. 'We'll have no peace until we get rid of the tinkers. That means getting rid of the camp.'

She's hoping to use an attack on the camp as an excuse to look for the package, Joe realised. And to harm Maggie.

'I say we should do something positive here and now.'

There were more cheers from a section of the crowd. But others had started to protest at the plan.

'Oh and what ought we to do to them? Wait until no decent people will want to live here or work here or open new factories?'

'Hey, look.' Peter Murphy pointed above the heads of the crowd. For a moment Joe thought he was pointing at him but it was Pat and Mr Mulligan that Peter had seen on the edge of the crowd. 'That's Pat O'Donoghue and one of his friends. They'll go and warn the tinkers.'

The crowd closed in around the two men, concealing them from view.

'Peter is right. They were skulking around, spying on us.' The red-haired woman jumped down and pushed her way towards the two captives. 'We can't let our plans be spoiled now.'

'Lock them up in the coalyard,' Peter Murphy said. 'Let someone stand guard.'

'That's the very thing,' the red-haired woman said. 'And then let those that are not with us mind their own business.'

There was no mistaking the threat in her voice. The majority of the crowd moved quickly away as Pat and Mr Mulligan were pushed forward towards the gates that enclosed a collection of ramshackle buildings, all that remained of a once thriving coal business. The granite weigh-house, however, was as complete as when it was built. It might have been designed especially to house Pat and Mr Mulligan.

The red-haired woman laughed in triumph as the outer gates were locked and a man selected to keep an eye on the prisoners. 'Off we go then, those who are with us.'

Joe's feet hardly touched the ground as he raced towards the camp. His arrival there took even the dogs by surprise. They scattered in all directions. Maggie and the O'Donoghues hurried towards him.

'There's trouble coming. Sean's sister is stirring up the people in the town against the camp. They're on their way here right now.'

Maggie made the sign of the cross.

Mick O'Donoghue turned to the other men. 'Get the women and children away from here. Some can go further up the road. Others can hide in the graveyard.'

'I'll not run,' Maggie said.

'We have enough to worry us without worrying about those that can't defend themselves. And it's not Joe's fight either. Let him take you down to the river. Bring a blanket with you.' He walked away, kicking clay onto the fires, ordering that lamps be turned off.

'He's wrong,' Joe said. 'It is my fight. Sean's sister and the Murphys are after the package that you hid in those trees. That's why they are attacking.'

'Go and get it then. If things turn out badly here we'll at least have some kind of weapon to use against them.'

Joe had forgotten how light and flexible the package was. He could easily fold it in two.

'What do you think is in it?' Maggie was by his side, a blanket folded over one arm, the crystal ball in her hands.

'I don't know. Let me carry those things for you. Does the crystal ball really tell you the future?'

'It's a question of belief,' Maggie said as she and Joe went through the gap in the hedge. 'Lead me over there to the corner.'

'Mr O'Donoghue said you were to go down to the river.'

'And where would the sense be in that? I want to see what happens. And I'd be no use way down at the river.'

'You're not going to get mixed up in it.'

'Nor do I intend to be run out of here by Sean and his sister.'

'Should I not try and get help?'

'From where?'

'Call the guards.'

'There's no-one on duty in Carroll's Bridge after eight o'clock at night. You'd have to telephone Kildare.'

'All right. I'll do that. I know where the telephone is and maybe I can help Pat and Mr Mulligan too. They're locked up in the coalyard.'

Chapter Eighteen

he safest way was through the grounds of Oakfield House and then along the river path towards the bridge.

The house looked more deserted than ever. What Ned had said about the Organiser's followers came back to Joe. They wouldn't all live in a world of ruined rooms and dark alleys. The Organiser himself must have a decent house. Maybe that was why he was so ruthless, to prevent himself ending up like Mollser and the Blind Man. Yet he helped to keep Mollser and the others poor by frightening them, making them totally dependent on him.

Joe crossed the only open bit of ground and reached the bridge. There was a ledge, part of the support structure of the bridge, within easy reach. The package might be safer there than with him. But what if it fell into the river? The

urge to open the package was almost impossible to resist. But before he could give in to the
temptation the red-haired woman came
marching out into the main street followed by
about fifteen people, far fewer than had origi-
nally been in the square. None the less, fifteen
men was a sizeable force for the tinkers to face.

Joe ducked out of sight as the crowd passed,
making encouraging noises to each other like
children afraid of shadows.

Once the sound had faded into the distance
Joe ran towards the market square. The only
person still there was the man on guard outside
the coalyard.

Joe forced the sound of Peter Murphy's voice
back into his mind, the long, slow vowels.
'Hello. Hello. You're to catch up with the
others.'

'What?' The man swayed slightly. It occurred
to Joe that he was slightly drunk. Maybe those
who followed the red-haired woman were too,
on drink supplied by the Murphys.

'Out towards the camp. I'll stay here.'

The man stared at Joe as though trying to
name him. Then he lurched out of the square
straight into the path of the grey car, which
swerved to avoid him and, in doing so, smashed
a rear light against a parked lorry. Then the car

straightened up and screeched to a stop outside Murphy's pub.

The man who got out of the driver's seat was the Organiser. Without so much as a glance around him he went into the pub.

Joe tried the lock on the coalyard gate. The wood was so rotted that it came away immediately. The weigh-house was a different proposition.

'It's me, Mr Mulligan. But I can't budge the door of this place.'

'Break the window. Find a stick or something.'

Better than a stick were the metal bars scattered around. Three good blows shattered the principal window through which a foreman would once have controlled the arrival and departure of delivery carts.

'There's a gang on its way to the camp but I got the package. Should we see what's in it?'

Joe tore the package open.

'It's money,' Pat said.

'But what kind of money? Dollars and English pounds? And all brand new. What does that suggest to you, Joe?'

'Forged money?'

'Exactly. The Organiser would seem to be getting out of the stolen credit card business and getting involved in a new venture all under his own control.'

'He's in Murphy's pub right now,' Joe said. 'He didn't lock the car.'

'And Sean?'

'No sign of him. Maybe he was dropped off to check on what's happening at the camp. Ned said the contents of the package could incriminate whoever it was found it. The Organiser has a broken rear light. Maggie and I think someone should call the guards.'

'I'll do that,' said Pat.

'And I'll take care of the package.' Before Mr Mulligan could object Joe took the money back and headed for the grey car. There was an overcoat on the back seat. Joe unfolded it slightly and pushed some of the money inside it. The remainder of the money he stuffed in his pocket and ran back toward Oakfield House.

Its front door was open just wide enough for Joe to slip inside without having to open it wider and risk making noise.

The hall and the stairs were like details from an old photograph, smudged and indistinct in the pale pools of moonlight that provided the only relief to the darkness.

Joe listened. The place was full of creaking sounds, of old wood worn out by the effects of damp air and raw winds.

A window rattled upstairs.

Then came a movement from the room at the end of the hall, the room that must be Sean's room.

Joe crept closer to it and listened. Two people were talking inside. But they did not dare put on a light. Their voices rose and fell as though they were arguing in a very intense way. Then suddenly a woman said in a very sharp manner, 'I don't trust you any longer. You've been playing both ends against the middle.'

Joe barely had time to step back into the shadows before the door was flung open and the woman passed down the hall. She flung the door wide open as Sean came running after her.

'Things'll be fine,' Sean said.

'Will they? That's what your sister said to me yesterday when I risked my whole future by driving down in the Organiser's car to see who was staying here.'

'And you think I haven't been taking even more chances than you?' Sean demanded.

'And why shouldn't you take more chances? What have you got to lose?' The woman turned her head and looked at Sean. A dapple of moonlight illuminated her face. It was the woman from the vegetable shop. 'But our

friends in Dublin will blame me if the Organiser walks away scot free. He already suspects
there's something on. Why else did he insist
that I turn up at the Place? He wanted to see if
Joe would be able to identify me. If we don't
destroy him now, we are at his mercy.'

'But what can I do?' Sean asked.

'I don't know. Think of something. I'll be late
for my lift back to Dublin. Results are what
count. If the Organiser gets control of the fake
money business we're all in deep trouble.' The
woman stepped out into the darkness and
crunched on the gravel towards the gate.

Sean flapped his hands despairingly, unde-
cided where to go next. Then he ran after the
woman.

'Now or never,' Joe thought.

Sean's room was no better furnished than
the one he had given to Ned. Clothes were
thrown around. On the table there was a two-
way walkie-talkie. The others would have
similar ones. On the mantelpiece there was an
old tin canister. Joe took the lid off. It was filled
with old betting slips. Joe pushed the remainder of the forged money in among them and
replaced the canister. Then he crept back to the
front door.

Sean was at the turn in the drive, still dithering as to what he should do next. Jacko would be like Sean in another twenty years if he wasn't helped.

Joe slid down the cliff face to the bank of the river. His eyes were used to the darkness now. The path was still firm in spite of the rain and easy to follow.

In St Michael's School the clock in the tower was like a time-telling moon. But the buildings were in darkness, their inhabitants unaware of the battle happening so close at hand.

A cloud of black smoke began to drift across the countryside carrying with it the smell of burning as Joe reached Maggie, who was now on her feet with the blanket wound about her like a shawl.

'What happened to you? I was getting worried.'

'I think I've fixed the Organiser and Sean. They'll both think that the woman from the vegetable shop did it.'

'What vegetable shop?'

'I'll explain later. Pat is telephoning the guards.'

'But will there be anything left for them to protect? Give me your arm. I might fall on this ground.'

As they crossed towards the gap in the hedge

they could see the silhouettes of fighting men and hear the crash of glass and crockery.

The O'Donoghues' caravan was being rocked back and forth until one last great heave turned it over completely.

'So you're here to do what the Murphys can't do by themselves,' Maggie said. Her words, spoken in so quiet a way and coming from outside the circle of violence, had a dramatic effect on the action.

The red-haired woman, stick in hand, recovered first. 'It's only one of them.'

'That's right. Just as you and your brother, Sean, were once like us too. Well, what's keeping you? Is my caravan not next on your list?'

'Don't listen to her. The lad that's with her attacked Peter Murphy and tried to steal the washing.'

'No, he didn't, and well you know it. But I suppose the rest of you will believe what you want to believe even if that means smashing this camp and leaving children with no shelter. But maybe they can find a ditch to lie in until you next need your fortune told or one of your wrecked cars to be taken away.'

'We're doing what's best for the town,' a man, suddenly shamefaced, said.

'You're doing what's best for the Murphys

and their friends, who'll ruin whoever they
choose. Ask your leader there what it is her
brother has been up to. Ask her who the Organiser is.'

'I don't know what she's talking about.'

'The guards'll be here soon now. Maybe
they'll have the answers.'

Mick O' Donoghue broke free of the men who
were holding him. 'You sent for the guards?'

'Pat did. Oh yes,' Maggie said to the mob.
'The men you locked up in the coalyard are free.
And the guards won't be too pleased by the
extra work you've given them this night.
Maybe someone ought to think of getting back
and warning the Murphys.'

There was another pause. Then suddenly
the mob vacated the campsite. And no-one
moved faster than the red-haired woman.

'Go and tell the others it's safe to come back,'
Maggie ordered. She smiled at Joe. 'You don't
want to be here either when the guards arrive.'

'I'm meeting Ned. I'll be all right.'

He ran back once more to the river. The
tinker dogs were barking as the business of
clearing the camp got under way. The countryside was a series of dark lines of trees and
hedges. The river by moonlight was mysterious
as the Mississippi in *Tom Sawyer*, the old dog-

eared copy of which would be back in its place on the library shelf. Ned had said to think of the present and not of the past. That just wasn't possible for Joe. He had to form connections between the two.

The bridge that the ghost-like herd of cows had crossed was in front of him, its lichens and mosses the colour of armour.

'Joe! Joe!' Brigid leaned over the bridge.

Joe scrambled up beside her. 'Where's Ned?'

'I'm here. The workmen's hut can't be reached by road. They've blocked the entrance with huge boulders. Brigid said that's to keep the travelling people out. How did things go at Carroll's Bridge?'

Joe told them. Ned didn't know whether to be pleased or upset at the risks Joe had taken. 'And you're sure it was the vegetable shop owner?'

'Yes. She's the link between the Organiser's street people and whoever else is involved.'

'Where's Alf Mulligan?'

'Gone back to Dublin maybe. He won't want to hang around until the guards arrive.'

'I should get his car back to him but I also need to know what's happened in the town.'

'Approach it from the Curragh,' Joe said.

'We seem to be forever sneaking around the

back way,' Ned said. 'But still things will be better once I've seen the solicitor tomorrow.'

'Do you still need to do that?'

'Yes. Then there's your future to decide.'

'I thought it was decided. This is like the conversation I had with Matron.'

'It's also probably like the conversation I'm going to have with Mr Lawford when I get back to Carringdon.'

'But where do I go?' Joe asked

'For the moment you'll have to stay here in that workmen's hut. I know it's lonely but it'll be daylight in less than seven hours.'

The main street of Carroll's Bridge was thronged with people and guards as Ned and Brigid drove through the town.

Ned slowed down and allowed Brigid to speak to one of the guards. 'What's going on?' she asked.

'A bit of local trouble. It's all under control. Drive carefully.'

At one corner Sean-of-the-Mountains was being questioned. A few yards further on a man was standing beside a grey car. More guards were looking at the tyres and the broken light. A sergeant was holding up an overcoat and examining it carefully.

'So that's the Organiser,' Ned said. 'The

man we are all supposed to fear. That was no idle boast of Joe's. He does seem to have taken care of him for the moment. Do you think it'd be safe to go back to the camp now so that I can have a chat with Maggie? The guards seem to be fully occupied here.'

Chapter Nineteen

oe didn't have much sleep. The mountains and the valley seemed to be full of sound all night long.

He tried counting sheep but that just reminded him of the sheep he had seen after Ned's arrest. When he did doze he dreamt that he was being driven along the motorway against a never-ending stream of cars, all of them with their headlights fully on.

At last he found some peace in just letting the events of the last two days drift through his mind as the river drifted towards the sea.

Ned and he had shared a whole new landscape, a whole new world of greyness split by sudden brightness, sudden movements, sudden understandings. They would soon sit around and talk things over, maybe in the company of Maggie and the

O'Donoghues. With Dingo as part of the scene. Or back in the Mulligans' snug little house. Or across the water in England.

The cough of the O'Donoghues' van was suddenly close at hand. Someone ran across the quarry. The door of the hut opened. Pat looked in. 'It's time for you to be off out of this.'

'Where's Ned?'

'Gone to Dublin with Mulligan's car. Maggie says you're not to worry. You're to stay with your aunt.'

'My aunt?'

'Maggie had the address and I drove over to her and asked if you could come and stay.'

'And she'll have me?'

'Yes, for a while anyway. Sean and the Organiser were arrested and Oakfield searched but we're not by any means in the clear yet.'

Joe settled down in the back of the van. A bright bar of golden light spread across the window as the sun rose over the Wicklow mountains. On the other side of them the sea would be reflecting the brilliant colours of a new day. The boat from Liverpool would be entering the mouth of the Liffey.

'Are Maggie and Brigid all right?'

'Grand. You can come and sit up here with me now if you like. We're clear of Carroll's Bridge.'

'Things keep repeating themselves, don't they?'

'But they don't always end in the same way,' Pat said.

Great flat fields were enclosed by well-kept hedges. On the horizon a goods train was going towards Galway. His aunt would tell him about Galway and growing up there.

'Only another twenty miles or so,' Pat said.

'As far as that? You mustn't have got home until all hours.'

'I like driving at night.'

The road twisted, doubling back on itself. Then it straightened out, empty and white.

'There's the car over there.' Pat did a U-turn and let Joe out.

The whole world seemed to shine as Joe reached the waiting car. 'Hello, Joe. I'm your Auntie Patricia. This is your Uncle Owen.'

Both of them smiled at him, their eyes filled with kindness.

'We'd best be off,' Owen said.

'I'll just say goodbye to Pat.'

But Pat was already gone.

'Never mind,' Patricia said. 'We'll go back

by way of Tullamore. That way it'll seem as though you came down from Dublin by bus. We'll say you're staying for a while until your father collects you.'

'I was in the papers last night.'

'We don't get the evening papers where we live. The farm is well away from things and the local town just a dot on the map. You'll have no need to meet people until it's all died down although Kitty is dying to see you, and Bart too.'

'Who are they?'

'Your cousins, of course.'

A father! An aunt! An uncle! Cousins!

Pat had been right. Things didn't always end in the same way.

Also by Tony Hickey

The "Spike and the Professor" books:

Spike and the Professor

Spike and the Professor...and Doreen at the Races

Spike, the Professor and Doreen in London

Children's
POOLBEG

Also by Tony Hickey

The "Brian the Leprechaun" books

Blanketland

Foodland

Legendland

Children's
POOLBEG